A LOVE STORY BOTH FRAGILE AND TIMELESS

Suddenly the door opened, and Marcie stood there, her hair cascading over her shoulders, the light from behind outlining every contour of her body.

He longed to rush over and crush her to him.

But it was Marcie who made the first move. Slipping off her negligee, she crossed the floor and stood in front of him, so close that the tips of her breasts touched his chest.

"I love you," she whispered.

* *

He had thought on that day nine years before, that he could never love her more. He had been wrong. He'd discovered that his love for the remarkable woman who had chosen to share life with him had grown. Through the bad times and the good, through the birth of their daughter, and the birth of their son, through every passing day—he had come to realize that the love he and Marcie shared was as infinite and as ever-expanding as the universe.

Without her . . .

A Novel by BARBARA BRETT

AVON
PUBLISHERS OF BARD, CAMELOT AND DISCUS BOOKS

BETWEEN TWO ETERNITIES is an original publication of Avon Books. This work has never before appeared in book form.

AVON BOOKS
A division of
The Hearst Corporation
959 Eighth Avenue
New York, New York 10019

Published by arrangement with the author:
Library of Congress Catalog Card Number: 78-61438
ISBN: 0-380-39925-3

First Avon Printing, December, 1978

Printed in the U.S.A.

To Hy, Jennifer, and Steven, who have turned my "fleeting gleam" into a warm and radiant glow.

In the sight of God, a thousand years are but as yesterday when it is past. Our life is but a fleeting gleam between two eternities.

From a traditional prayer
for the Jewish New Year

Chapter One

Attending a stuffy faculty party was not the way Robert and Marcie Silver would have chosen to spend the tenth anniversary of the day they met, but, with Robert's tenure hearings scheduled for the following term, they had no alternative. Besides, they were young and strong and sure that they had many years ahead of them in which to commemorate the occasion properly. There was no way they could have known that this was their last year together.

So they left a baby-sitter in charge of five-year-old Rachel and three-year-old Benjie and set off for the home of Roscoe Bradcliff, who evidently believed that if he plied his colleagues with sufficient drink, he could float their votes for the chairmanship of the English department into his port.

The elevator in their apartment house was out of order once again, so they walked down the five double flights of stairs that led to the lobby, where they paused as Robert lit his pipe. It would have been difficult to single Robert out in a group of other men in their mid-thirties. Of average height and weight, he wore his sandy hair fashionably long and his beard fashionably short in the manner of men in the seventies; but, though his wire-framed glasses gave him a studious look, they did not mask the humor that lurked in his gray eyes. Marcie, too, might not have stood out in a crowd of beauties, though she was an attractive woman of thirty-two whose dark eyes shone with intelligence and laughter. Yet, when the two stood together, an aura of their love and oneness seemed to surround them, often making others pause and take notice.

Robert drew on his pipe, and a spark puffed out of it, alighting on his beard. Quickly, Marcie reached up to brush it off.

"Hey, watch it!" she teased. "You don't have to prove you're the light of my life by going up in flame. I need you."

"Don't worry," he said. "I plan to stick around for at least another hundred years."

"Swell—and after that, we can grow old together."

Robert laughed, but the thought crossed his mind, as it had more than once since they'd fallen in love, that he was glad wives usually outlived their husbands. For him, life without Marcie would be no life at all.

He took her hand, and they walked out into the April evening. Though earlier the air had glowed with the sunny promise of spring, the remembered chill of winter had sneaked back under cover of the evening shadows, and, instinctively, Robert and Marcie hugged their coats a little closer.

Having long since tired of keeping local car thieves supplied—two used Chevrolets had disappeared within months of their purchase—they had for some time remained voluntarily dependent upon public transportation. Now they headed for the subway along a street that, like the house they lived in, had gone to seed. When they had married nine years before, the neighborhood—formerly a prestigious one that surrounded the beautiful Brooklyn Botanic Garden, the Brooklyn Museum, and the main branch of the Brooklyn Public Library—had only just begun to show signs of crumbling, and they had felt lucky to have found a large, roomy, rent-controlled apartment there. Over the years, however, crime, along with its henchman, neighborhood blight, had begun to put more and more of a claim upon the area as its own private turf. Robert and Marcie would have liked to move, but, city people at heart, they found the thought of fleeing to the suburbs stultifying; and, with rent control no longer in existence, moving to an apartment, even halfway comparable to the one they occupied, in a safer, more elegant neighborhood would have meant financial disaster. So they tried to be cheerful about the fact that they were trapped where they were for the foreseeable future.

Marcie took a deep breath of the chilly air. "The weather was something like this the day we met," she said. "Remember?"

Robert gave her a sidelong look. "How can I remember that when I had eyes only for you?"

She shook her head in mock despair. "Oh, brother! The ten years haven't done much to improve your line either!"

Smiling, but silent, they walked on toward the subway, each lost in memories of that day ten years before. Marcie, who was an undergraduate art student back then, had stationed herself across the street from New York's luxurious Plaza Hotel, intent upon capturing its elegance in her sketchbook, but she had captured instead Robert, the passer-by who had paused to kibitz.

Robert, who was then winding up his studies for his master's degree in English literature, had never been particularly interested in art, but he did like the shape and form of the artist before him. Hands in his dungaree pockets, he peered over her shoulder for a while, and when she pointedly ignored him, he finally ventured to say, "You don't mind if I watch, do you?"

She shrugged, saying, "It's a free country," her hand never missing a stroke. Then she continued to ignore him.

After a moment, he tried again: "I like your blues and greens."

That caught her attention. "I'm using *charcoal.*"

She looked at him as though she thought he was crazy, but, at least, she looked at him.

"I know," he said, his gaze flipping over her.

Realizing he was referring to her jeans and green sweatshirt, she rolled her eyes heavenward and, possibly addressing a pigeon that was heading for Central Park, said, "Spare me!"

The pigeon, evidently more interested in peanuts than in dungaree-clad damsels in distress, did not interrupt its flight to come to her aid, and Robert continued to hover at her elbow—an elbow that began to move up and down more vigorously as it followed the movements of her hand across the page.

"Your style reminds me a lot of Renoir's middle period—before he was influenced by Cézanne."

"I don't think Renoir was *ever* influenced by Cézanne." Her eyes never left her work.

"By Picasso then—or Andy Warhol."

"Come on, will you? I'm trying to concentrate. This sketch is a homework assignment."

"What if you should flunk? Would your teacher make you copy the Mona Lisa ten times?"

Her eyes still didn't leave her work, but the corners of her mouth began to twitch upward. "Probably the Sistine Chapel. He's very tough."

"I think this picture is going to be too good for your teacher. How about selling it to me?"

"Just before you came along, the art director of the Metropolitan Museum offered me a quarter of a million for it. Can you top that?"

"Easy! Of course, I'll have to consult my banker

first. In the meantime, can I make a down payment by taking you to lunch?"

"I'm sorry, but I don't lunch with strangers."

"Not even if they're millionaires?"

The smile she had been trying to suppress bubbled over into a laugh. "With millionaires, I usually make an exception."

"I think that's very wise. May I suggest the Automat?"

"The Automat?" Her eyes danced with mischief. "Why not the Plaza? It's right across the street, and I thought that was where all you millionaires hung out."

He sighed. "The Plaza holds no thrill for me anymore. I eat there morning, noon, and night. All that rich food is finally affecting my stomach. My Park Avenue physician has ordered me to switch to the simple fare that can be found only in places like the Automat."

"Well, we certainly can't go against your physician's orders," she said, closing her sketchbook and putting her charcoal into her pocket.

Taking her pad from her, he slipped it under his arm. "If I'm to be your patron, I think I should tell you my name."

"No—let me guess. You must be one of the Marx Brothers."

"You're close. I'm Robert Silver, though people often mistake me for Robert Redford. I guess you've noticed the resemblance too." He offered her a view of his profile.

"Sure. It's the first thing I noticed about you. I said to myself, 'Look, there's Robert Redford. I thought I read in Rona Barrett's column that he was making a movie in China. A lot she knows! He's right here in New York, and if I play my cards right, maybe he'll take me to lunch at the Automat.' "

"Actually, I've heard he's a food faddist. Probably the most he would have done for you would have been to buy you a cup of green tea. You're lucky it was me instead."

"Talk about narrow escapes!"

They strolled over to the Automat on Fifty-ninth Street, and there, over fish cakes and spaghetti, they began to fall in love.

Since they were both students with very little means, their romance had been a frugal—but delightful—one. They'd had no need for expensive entertainment, though—not with all the joy they found in each other. They visited museums and galleries, where Marcie taught Robert to share her love for art. They went to free lectures and readings, where Robert shared with her his world of words. Arms around each other, they strolled the city streets. Hand in hand, they sat on park benches. And, always, they talked—sharing with each other their thoughts, their beliefs, their hopes, their fears, and their dreams as they had never been able to share them with anyone before. It had been more than a sharing; it had been a merging of mind and heart and soul—a living, growing process that they knew was vital to each of them and that they realized bound them together for life.

They married that December, and their first domestic activity upon moving into the dilapidated one-room apartment they had rented in the East Village had been to hang Marcie's sketch of the Plaza over the studio couch that served as their bed. The sketch had had the place of honor over their bed ever since.

Their first five years had been a struggle. At the start, Robert worked full time while Marcie finished her studies for her degree. That accomplished, they reversed their roles that June, and Marcie went to work as an illustrator for an advertising agency while Robert studied for his doctorate in English literature.

Now the hard times were over. For nearly five years, Robert had been teaching at Seward College, one of the branches of the City University, and Marcie, who had left the agency to raise their children, had turned the spare room of their apartment into a studio, and did occasional free-lance jobs. Money was far from overabundant, but life was good. As long as they had each other, life would always be good.

Pausing at the entrance to the subway, Robert knocked the ashes from his pipe. "I have a great idea: Let's ditch Bradcliff's bash and go someplace where we can be by ourselves."

"That has to be one of the nicest—and one of the dumbest—ideas you've ever come up with. If you don't show at Bradcliff's party, you'll be on his enemies list forever."

"Not necessarily. He has to be nice to me. He wants my vote for department chairman."

"But the election will be over long before your tenure hearing comes up. That will give him plenty of time to brood over old wounds. Besides, I thought you were voting for Tilman."

"Probably, but neither he nor Tilman knows that."

"For a professor, you're turning into quite a politician."

"Unfortunately, to be a professor and stay one, one has to turn into a politician."

"Which is exactly why we have to turn up at all Bradcliff's bashes—and Tilman's."

Robert sighed and started down the subway stairs. "Screw them both."

"The thing is," Marcie said, "to keep them both from screwing you."

They sat on a bench on the subway platform to await their train. Marcie leaned her head back against the wall and closed her eyes.

Robert peered at her. "You okay? You look a little pale."

She shrugged. "My lunch disagreed with me. My stomach's been a little queasy on and off all day."

"Why didn't you tell me? I'd have called Bradcliff and cancelled."

"Let's not go through that again. That's exactly why I didn't tell you. Besides, there's nothing like one of these faculty parties to test and strengthen one's intestinal fortitude."

"We can still get out of it."

"You're looking for excuses," she teased.

"You're damn right I am," he said, laughing.

"Well, forget it. I feel well enough to face the whole boring crew."

"Even Professor Graystone?"

"Well, *almost* the whole crew."

Their train pulled into the station, and they boarded it, laughing.

Roscoe Bradcliff and his shadow of a wife occupied the second floor of a renovated brownstone in the east Eighties, where they surrounded themselves with the anthologies of works of famous authors that Roscoe compiled and edited. The buzzing of voices that drifted through his door as Robert and Marcie approached it indicated that the party was already in full swing.

Robert rang the doorbell.

A few seconds later, the door swung open, and Bradcliff, who attempted to espouse the fashions of youth physically as well as intellectually, stood before them in burgundy bell-bottoms and a pink, flower-print, wide-sleeved shirt.

"Welcome, *shalom, bienvenue!*" he said, giving Robert a hearty slap on the back. "So glad you could make it to our little get-together."

"It's good to be here," Robert said. He smiled warmly at the frail, graying woman who was hovering behind Bradcliff. "How are you, Mrs. Bradcliff?"

"I'm fine, thank you," Mrs. Bradcliff ventured.

"Yes, yes, they can see that. Why don't you take their coats?"

"We'll take care of them," Marcie said.

"Melba wouldn't hear of it, would you, Melba?"

Melba nodded that of course she wouldn't hear of it and ducked away with the coats.

Placing an arm around each of them, Bradcliff headed them away from his wife and into the heart of the party. "Go on over to the bar and get yourselves something to drink. Make yourselves comfortable. Everyone's here."

Everyone was the entire English department, with the exception of Tilman and the few professors who had sufficient tenure and reputation to swear their allegiance to him openly before the election.

The doorbell rang, and Bradcliff gave their shoulders a parting squeeze. "Go ahead. Get yourselves a drink. I'll get back to you."

"Not if I see him first!" Marcie whispered as he walked away.

"After a few drinks, he'll look better." Robert took her hand and headed toward the bar, which was knee-deep in scholarship.

"Oh, lord!" Marcie whispered. "There's Professor Graystone. He looks half-crocked already. Any minute now, he'll start reading his poetry."

"*Coraggio!* I'll make us doubles."

They took their drinks and settled themselves on the sofa.

"Would you like an hors d'oeuvre?" Melba Bradcliff looked as if she half-expected them to slap away the tray she was tentatively extending toward them.

"Thank you, I'd love one," Marcie said, reaching for one with an olive-topped, yellowish-orange spread. She bit into it. "This is delicious! How do you make it?"

Melba shrank into herself with a nervous laugh. "Oh, I never make the hors d'oeuvres. Roscoe says I'd just botch them. We always get them from a caterer."

"Well, then you certainly know how to pick caterers," Marcie said.

"Oh, no! Roscoe does that. He's much better at planning parties than I am."

"Melba! There are more coats to be seen to!" Bradcliff's voice cut across the room.

For a moment, Melba's eyes darted from the tray in her hands to her husband and back again in confusion.

"Melba!"

Quickly, she placed the tray on a nearby table. "Excuse me, please," she whispered and scurried away.

"That son of a bitch!" Robert said. "If he had a dog, he'd probably kick it."

Marcie's eyes grew sad. "A dog, at least, might turn on him and bite him one day. I think he's long since robbed his wife of the ability to do that." She handed Robert her hors d'oeuvre. "You want this? It's awful. Tastes like yellow plaster of paris."

He laughed and slipped it into an ashtray. "And

you would have eaten the whole thing if she had stood there any longer, wouldn't you?"

"Well, it's time someone made the poor woman feel she's good for something, even if it is just handing out yellow plaster of paris."

"I see you've made yourselves comfortable. That's fine, fine." Bradcliff had made his way over to them again. "How do you like the old homestead?"

Robert looked around at the sharp angles of the starkly modern black and white furniture. The apartment was decorated with all the warmth of a hospital operating room. "It's certainly very now," he said.

"And that's where it's at, boy. That's where it's at." There was room for him on the sofa, but he settled instead on its arm, a perch from which he could look informal yet condescending. "And that's where we've got to be in our work as well as in our lives. Of course, this is a party, and no one wants to talk shop, but you know what I mean," he said with a wink. "There are those stick-in-the-muds who have never had a new idea in their heads and who would like to keep the whole English department in the Dark Ages. But we're not going to let them get away with that, are we?"

Robert managed to be sipping his drink so that he didn't have to answer.

"Exactly!" Bradcliff said, getting up. "Well, enjoy yourselves. I'll get back to you again."

He had no sooner walked away than Katherine Marish zeroed in on them. A short redhead with a voluptuous figure, she looked and dressed as if she belonged on a centerfold of *Playboy* rather than behind a lectern, but she was all scholar from her *summa cum laude* degree from Barnard to the thesis on "Henry James and Evolution of the Parenthetical Clause" that would soon win her her Ph.D.

"Marcia! How good to see you again!" she said, extending a cool, well-manicured hand. "What have you been doing with yourself lately?"

"Oh, wiping noses, applying Band-Aids."

"Now you can't fool me!" She tossed her head back and laughed. "Robert has told me how hard you work on your little drawings. I'll bet you're working on something right now."

"As a matter of fact, I'm illustrating a pamphlet for the Anti-Smoking League."

"How fascinating!"

"Not really, unless you happen to get turned on drawing cross sections of diseased lungs."

"Oh, come now! I'm sure you find a way to get some self-expression into it!"

"I understand that the way I render smoke curling from a cigarette is something to behold."

"You see!" Katherine said in the tone of an adult who has just scored a point with a child. She took Robert's hand in an effort to pull him to his feet. "I have to borrow your husband for a little while. I need him to settle an argument about Fitzgerald. Robert's the only person whose word I'll take on Fitzgerald."

With a sigh, Robert rose. "Be back in a minute, honey."

Marcie nodded.

Katherine wound a possessive arm through Robert's. "I hope you'll send me one of those little pamphlets when they're ready," she called over her shoulder as she led him away.

"Oh, I will!" The smile on Marcie's lips matched Katherine's, but the mischief in her eyes indicated that if the pamphlet were to arrive at Katherine's house at all, it might be through a closed window, wrapped around a brick. She took a long swallow of her drink.

The sofa sagged under the weight of Arthur Dowley, who had been teaching at the college for thirty years and who, for some obscure offense in the remote past, had been on the shit list of every chairman of the English department for the past twenty-five. His vote, however, could never be overlooked, and so he received grudging invitations to every pre-election get-together.

He took a swallow of what was obviously only one in a long line of drinks. "Look at that shithead," he said, nodding toward Bradcliff, "prancing around, talking about how *exhausted* he is from working on his latest anthology." He fixed a bleary eye on Marcie. "Do you know what parts of a man get most worn out working on an anthology?"

"What parts?"

"His ass and his index finger. All he has to do is select an author, then sit himself down in front of a card catalogue in his local library and make a list of all the works by that author. He gets copies of the works, strings them all together, and, *voilà!*, an anthology."

Marcie laughed. "Sounds like instant scholarship."

"Exactly. Just add a few lines of bullshit for a forward and mix." His thick, graying brows lowered over his eyes in a scowl. "What a bunch of phonies we all are, trying to build reputations for brilliance and cleverness on works created by minds far more brilliant and clever than our own. There are damn few who can see the situation in perspective—who are in this business for the love of teaching and the love of *what* they're teaching. You happen to be lucky enough to be married to one of them."

Marcie smiled. "And to be sitting next to one of them too."

"No." He gulped down the remainder of his drink. "I lost all my perspective long ago. I'm too bitter to offer accurate judgments, and if you're smart, you'll keep that in mind whenever you talk to me."

"The only people whose judgment I'd deem worth trusting are those who have the wisdom to mistrust what they say."

A grin traced its way across his face, then was lost in a scowl as someone began to clank a spoon against a glass at the bar.

It was Professor Graystone, his gray curls bobbing, his plump body rigid with the effort of pretending not to contain too much gin. "Your attention, everybody!" he was saying through his long, aquiline nose. "Your attention, please! I have a treat for you. I've written a poem in honor of our good host."

"Oh, Christ!" Dowley grunted. "I'll need another drink for this." He got to his feet. "Can I get you one?"

Marcie shook her head.

He bent down, peering at her through his bloodshot eyes. "Say, are you okay? You look a little green around the gills."

Marcie closed her eyes a second, her long, slender fingers moving up to her neck. "I think my drink disagreed with me."

"Well, if it didn't, Graystone's poem certainly will. Why don't you pry Katherine's hooks out of your husband and get him to take you home?"

"I think I'll do that." She rose a little unsteadily. "But first I'd better find the bathroom. Do you know where it is?"

"Second door off the hall. Can you make it all right?"

"Yes, thanks." She began working her way out of the room.

"I call this poem 'To Reginald,' " Professor Graystone was saying, "because Roscoe is really not a terribly poetic name. But we all know I mean you, Roscoe dear. Now to begin: 'Behind ivory brow there teems a mind/Fraught with knowledge of humankind. . . .' "

Unaware that he had long since lost his audience, Professor Graystone was on his third poem—

a Petrarchan sonnet in praise of T. S. Eliot—when Marcie emerged from the bathroom, her face pale, her eyes searching the room for Robert. He was still standing in the small circle Katherine had shepherded him off to, his arm still held tightly in her grasp. His face lit up as he spotted Marcie's approach, but the pleasure in his eyes turned to concern by the time she reached his side.

"Honey, what is it?"

"I'm not feeling too well. I think we'd better go."

He disentangled himself from Katherine's hold, collected their coats, and made his excuses to Bradcliff. Then he led Marcie out into the cool April evening.

"Does your stomach feel up to a taxi?" he asked, slipping his arm around her waist.

She leaned her head against his shoulder. "Not yet. The air feels good, though. Let's walk a while."

They walked over to Fifth Avenue, then headed south. A light rain had begun to fall, and Robert reached over with his free hand, slipping the hood of her rain-or-shine coat over her dark hair.

"You should have told me sooner that you weren't feeling well."

"I didn't know sooner. It crept up on me suddenly—while I was talking to Dowley."

Robert laughed. "That will do it every time."

"No, really! I rather like him. He's bitter as hell, but I get the impression that he has a right to be. Besides, it's hard to find fault with a misanthrope who's down on everyone except your husband."

"He likes me?"

She snuggled closer. "Said you were the only perceptive nonphony in the bunch."

"I don't know that I owe my nonphoniness as much to perception as I do to laziness. I've never been able to see any point in knocking my brains out to make some obscure point of scholarship in some erudite quarterly."

"Sure, you're lazy! That's why you're knocking yourself out on the Wharton biography."

"That's different. Anyway, I'm glad to hear the old bastard likes me. Though it's not the most popular sentiment back where we hail from, I have to admit that I rather like him too."

"Why is everybody so down on him?"

Robert shrugged. "No one in our department talks about it or seems to know, but an old-timer in the history department once told me that when Dowley was first starting out, he made the mistake of giving the rough of a paper he was writing on Chaucer to his department head for criticism. The guy found so little to criticize that he plagiarized it, published it under his own name, and greatly enhanced his own reputation. Dowley made a stink, but couldn't prove a thing, since he'd been naive enough to let his only copy of the paper out of his hands. The department head had a big reputation, prestige, and pull, so, naturally, everyone rallied around him—they needed him more. Dowley was left out in the cold, and his bitterness has kept him there. The fact that his wife ran off with one of his colleagues a year or so later didn't serve to sweeten his disposition any either."

"The poor guy." Marcie shuddered a little. "He was really rather sweet to me. A lot of people wouldn't have noticed that I wasn't feeling well, but he did. You know, I think he would have walked me to the bathroom and held my head for me if I had let him."

Smiling, Robert tightened his arm around her. "Just as long as he doesn't want to hold any other part of you when you're feeling okay."

Marcie laughed. "Just because you're a dirty old man, don't go thinking everybody else is. Speaking of dirty old men and dirty young women—how come Katherine Marish can never keep her cotton-pickin' hands off you?"

"Because I'm so irresistible." Laughing, he dodged away from her quick nudge in the ribs. "Actually, she gives me a pain. She's falling hopelessly in love with the most dazzling member of the faculty—herself—and she's a bit of a bore about it. I'm sorry I always seem to get dragged off somewhere, leaving you stranded, when we come to these things."

"Don't be. The same thing happens to you when we go to a gallery opening or some other arty get-together."

"I know, but, at least, when it happens to me, a braless wonder usually comes to my rescue—not some bitter old man."

"Go soak your head," she laughed.

"I am soaking it—or hadn't you noticed that it's raining?"

"You want to head for the subway?"

"Not unless you do."

She shook her head.

They walked on in the easy silence of friends and lovers, watching the headlights of passing cars isolate the rain into tiny particles that sparkled like a shower of baguettes, listening to the soft slap of their wet shoes on the glistening sidewalk. They had no need to speak nor even to think. All that was necessary for each of them was to feel the nearness of the other. That was their strength and their joy.

At Seventy-seventh Street, Robert guided their steps toward Lexington Avenue and the subway. He paused a moment before they descended, turning to look down at her.

"I wish I could paint you this way," he said, "with the rain on your face and the dampness curling your hair."

"Hey, painting's my territory. Don't try to muscle in on it." Gently, she caressed his chin. "I was planning to immortalize this wet beard on canvas myself."

"Well, I wouldn't want to compete on your own grounds. I'll get Professor Graystone to help me with an ode."

"Paint, please! I'll lend you my supplies."

Smiling, he reached into his pocket for tokens. "You ready to head home?"

She nodded, and he noticed for the first time how heavy her eyes looked.

"That sounds good," she said. "I'm very, very tired."

She slept on his shoulder all the way back to Brooklyn.

Chapter Two

April warmed to the springtime sun, its rains washing away the last chilling vestiges of the brisk March winds. At school, Robert taught his classes and attempted to avoid the politicking faculty as much as possible. Now that the election was drawing nearer, the partisans of both camps were zeroing in on all members of the staff who had not yet declared themselves. Tilman's clique rallied around the banner of scholarship, proclaiming that Tilman would crown the department with new laurels, using his prestige as one of the country's foremost Johnsonian authorities to lure other well-known scholars to the staff as visiting or permanent professors. Bradcliff's circle waved the flag of change, declaring it was time the department was modernized along the informal lines of student demands, hinting that Bradcliff's influence with people who had influence might bring some much needed foundation money into the department. Believing both men to be pedants at opposite poles, Robert leaned toward Tilman as the lesser evil. To declare himself, however, would have been both foolhardy and dangerous, demolishing his chances for tenure if the opposing party won. So he tried to avoid both groups, and listened amicably when all escape routes were blocked.

In the meantime, he taught and gathered material for his biography. He was also working on a short piece on Beerbohm's satire, hoping it would ease the pressure both Tilman and Bradcliff were exerting on him to have yet another paper published before the question of his tenure came up for review in the fall.

He was so engrossed in his own work that he wasn't fully aware that Marcie was still not feeling entirely well. He had noticed that she was more tired and pale than usual, but, because she always insisted that she was fine when he asked, he attributed it to the fact that she'd been nursing both children through spring colds. It wasn't until late in the month that he realized there might be more to it than that. That was the evening both children greeted him at the door with the exciting news that Mommy had gone to sleep on the floor.

"Just for a minute," Rachel elaborated.

"But it was scary until she woke up," Benjie said.

Robert put them down and headed for the kitchen. "Hey! What's going on?"

Marcie turned from the stove where she'd been stirring a pot of spaghetti. The steam from cooking made the short ends of her hair cling to her cheeks in tight little curls.

"Everything!" she cried, running to hug him. "You'll never guess who called today."

"The curator of the Met. He wants the originals of your illustrations for the anti-smoking pamphlet."

"You're close. The editor of Bambi Books. They like the samples I submitted. They want me to illustrate some books for them."

"That's great!"

"Great? It's stupendous!" Her eyes sparkled. "The whole illustrating field is open to me now. And after I've done a few books, I know I'll be able to get a one-man show. Oh, Bob! This is only the beginning!"

He pulled her close, his heart swelling with love and pride. "You're on your way to the top, sweetheart," he said in his best Humphrey Bogart voice.

She nestled against his chest a moment, then stiffened and pulled away, but not before he caught the glint of tears in her eyes. "Oh, hell! What's the use? I've had a lovely afternoon pretending, but that's all it is—pretending. I'll never be able to fulfill that contract Bambi's offering, never be able to have that one-man show. At least, not for years and years. And by then it may be too late."

She slumped down at the table, buried her head

in her arms and began to cry. "Damn it! I think I'm pregnant again!"

A rush of emotions staggered Robert, but not one of them was joy. The predominant feeling was a cold, slow-sinking dread. They'd planned to limit their family to two. Where would he get the money to support and educate a third? Moonlighting in the School of General Studies, giving up the precious time he needed to research the papers he had to publish if his career was ever to get off the ground? Where would he get the strength to help Marcie nurse another child through its illnesses and anxieties? Where would he get the stamina to guide it through childhood and adolescence, giving it the moral and emotional support it would need to survive in a world that was growing more insane with each passing day?

"God! Are you sure?"

"It's too soon to be positive, but, God knows!, I've got all the signs—nausea, sleepiness, headaches. I even blacked out for a few seconds this afternoon."

"I know. The kids told me when I came in."

"The little finks! I told them to keep it a secret."

"You know Benjie. As long as he whispers, he thinks it's still a secret."

Tears welled up in her eyes again, and her lower lip began to quiver. "Oh, Bob! What are we going to do? Why did it have to happen *now*—just when we're getting over the hump of the toddler stage with Benjie, just when things were beginning to go so well for us?"

He sat down and reached across the table for her hand. "You don't have to have it if you don't want to, you know."

"It's funny, isn't it?" she said, her smile turning to sadness in her eyes. "Here I am—the gal who marched for liberalized abortion laws, who practically stormed Albany—and yet, when it gets down to cases for myself, I'm not sure I'd want to go through with it."

"You don't believe in it anymore?"

"Oh, I still believe that it's the right of every woman to make her own decision. It's just that I'm not sure I could do it myself. If it was a rapist's child, I wouldn't think twice about it, but . . ." Her hand tightened on his and her chin began to tremble. "But this is your baby, Bob. I don't think I could do that to your baby. Still, starting all over again with bottles and diapers and sleepless nights, with tearing yourself apart inside because you don't know why your baby's crying or where he hurts and you love him so much and you long to help him and comfort him but you don't know how—I don't know how I can face up to that again either."

Gently, he pushed her hair back from her face. "Let's wait till we find out if you're really pregnant before we start worrying about what to do. Maybe you're not pregnant at all. Maybe it's just some crazy kind of virus. Make an appointment with the obstetrician tomorrow. See what he says."

"I can't. He'll tell me it's too soon."

"Too soon, hell! Surely there are tests he can take. Call him and insist that he see you soon."

She nodded.

He got up and slipped his arm around her shoulders. "Then, if you are pregnant—well, we'll work it out whatever way you want. If you want to have the baby, I'll help you all I can. Maybe I can get some night classes so we can hire someone to help out. You're not going to have to pass up this chance from Bambi. I promise you that."

Sighing, she relaxed against him. "You always know how to make things seem better. That's part of why I love you so much."

"And I thought it was because I had the cutest beard this side of the Mississippi."

"Nope. Only the scratchiest one."

Suddenly Rachel ran into the room. "Ooooh! What smells?"

"Our dinner!" Marcie cried, rushing to the stove. "Oh! Just look at that!"

"Spaghetti crisps," Robert said. "My favorite! Come on, we'll all go out and get some hamburgers to go with it."

He managed to keep the tension from creeping back that evening, and he tried to keep it at bay during the week that passed before Marcie's appointment with the obstetrician.

It was difficult, though, because he was under so much pressure of his own at the college. The declared parties for Bradcliff and Tilman were now fairly evenly split, and both candidates were breathing down the necks of the undeclared. Both men regarded impartiality with suspicion and had spies among the unallied—persons who, though posing as undecided, had secretly pledged themselves to one or the other and who attempted to elicit the true inclinations of the secretive.

Robert had a strong suspicion that Katherine was one of those spies—a suspicion she seemed intent on proving well founded when he ran into her in the faculty lounge on the day Marcie had her doctor's appointment. Almost immediately, she began blasting Bradcliff, but, upon receiving no strong positive response from him, she switched tactics and launched into an attack on Tilman.

"I hear that he's claiming that if he's elected he'll engage God as a visiting lecturer," she sneered.

"I'm not sure of God's background in English and American lit," Robert said, "but I imagine He'd do a hell of a job livening up our Bible course."

Emitting her well-practiced tinkling laugh, she slipped her arm through his and led him toward the coffee table. "Joking aside," she said, her voice as intimate as if they were in a bedroom, "whom do you really prefer? Knowing how you think would help me decide."

"I was about to say the same thing to you."

Her glance shifted away. "I just can't make up my mind. They're both admirable men—"

"They're both horses' asses," a caustic voice cut in.

Katherine and Robert turned and saw Professor

Dowley sloshing a piece of cake around in his coffee cup.

Katherine raised a well-shaped eyebrow. "Really, Arthur! Your language sometimes makes it difficult for one to remember that you're a Chaucerian scholar."

"It shouldn't. Chaucer used a hell of a lot worse." He took a bite of his soggy cake. "And since when don't you know whom you're voting for? Seems to me, every time I've looked up lately I've seen you sucking around Bradcliff and his bunch."

"Really!"

Robert took advantage of the preliminaries for the oncoming battle to disengage himself from Katherine's grasp and head for the coffee urn. He had barely added his sugar and cream when Katherine appeared at his elbow again.

"That man is impossible. I don't know why they keep him on!"

"He's well tenured, he's one of the best Chaucerian scholars around, and his students like him."

"But what his colleagues think of him should count for something."

"If what our colleagues really thought of us counted for anything, we'd all be working as garbagemen." He offered her the cup of coffee he had just prepared, but she shook her head.

"What I really need after that run-in is something stronger. If you've finished with classes for the day, why don't we stop off somewhere for a drink?"

"Sorry, but I have a conference with a student in ten minutes."

"Students give me a pain."

"But where would we be without them?"

"After that, then?"

He shook his head. "No. I have to get home."

"Don't tell me Marcie keeps such stringent tabs on you." She was only half joking.

"No. *I* keep such stringent tabs on Marcie." He managed to put his cup down and turn away without laughing. Then he headed for his office, leaving her to mull it over.

The meeting—with a barely literate but strongly motivated freshman—turned out to be more a lesson in remedial reading and writing than a conference, and it exceeded the ten minutes that were supposed to be allotted to it by fifty. Finally, recommending intensive study in summer school, Robert rushed out of his office intent on heading home.

Katherine just happened to be leaving her office at the same moment. "That must have been some conference," she said. "You look as though you could use a drink after all."

"I'm sure Marcie will have one waiting." Then to soften the bluntness of the remark, he added, "You'll have to come over one evening and sample some of her sours—they're great."

"I'd love to," she said, but her smile looked as though she'd already sucked one too many lemons.

He took a taxi home, but the extravagance was all for an anticlimax.

Marcie was seated on the edge of the tub in the

bathroom, applying a Technicolor Band-Aid to one of Benjie's imaginary wounds.

"He's not sure." She answered Robert's question before he had a chance to ask it. "He said it doesn't really look like I am, but he took some tests."

He admired Benjie's wound. "When will he know?"

She shrugged. "He's off tomorrow. I have to call back the day after." With a pat on the rear, she sent Benjie on his way.

Extending a hand, Robert helped her to her feet. "What's two more days? They'll be over before you know it."

Marcie smiled and rubbed her cheek against his beard. "Wanna bet?"

She was right. The two days passed with the speed of tortoise-drawn dogcarts.

At the end of the second, Robert found Marcie in her studio when he came home. The children were splashing away with water colors in a corner she kept reserved for them, and she sat at her sketchboard, working on an illustration for a Bambi book.

"Well?"

She shook her head no. "If I'd waited till today, I wouldn't have had to take the tests and could have saved us thirty dollars."

"So that worry's over."

She gave a little shrug, averting his gaze.

There was a smudge of charcoal on her cheek, and he walked over and began rubbing at it gently with his thumb. "Want to know something? I'm kind of disappointed. I was getting used to the idea."

As she looked up at him, he thought he caught a quick glint of tears in her eyes. "Want to know something? Me too. Now, isn't that the damnedest thing?"

She leaned her head against his chest, and he stood there for a moment, silently running his hand over her hair.

Suddenly, he stiffened, a fresh worry worming its way through to his consciousness. "If you're not pregnant, what's been making you sick?"

"I don't know. Maybe a virus. Maybe my hormones were out of kilter for a while, and now they'll straighten themselves out. Anyway, Taubman says that if it keeps up, I should go to our internist and let him check it out. So we'll wait and see."

They waited and saw through the last few days of April and the beginning of May. Around the time Bradcliff was elected department chairman, Marcie's nausea and tiredness returned.

"Maybe they're sympathy pains," she teased Robert. "You always said that the thought of Bradcliff as chairman made you sick."

"Not that sick. I guess the department will survive."

She reached for his hand, her eyes searching his. "And what about you? Will you survive?"

"We won't know till the fall, when my tenure hearings come up. The election was so close that it's pretty obvious who voted for whom. Bradcliff's smile when I congratulated him could have frozen over an active volcano."

"But he doesn't carry so much weight by himself, does he?"

"No, but he has friends in administration and on all the committees that have a say on tenure."

"And he can screw you through them, is that it?"

"It's been done. But I'm not going to worry about it. He's teaching summer school this year and I'm not, so he'll have the whole summer to build up new animosities and forget about old ones."

"And if he doesn't?"

Robert laughed. "We always land on our feet, don't we?"

She rubbed her rear. "Or on something with sufficient padding to absorb the shock."

"Exactly. That's why we're not going to waste any time worrying about it now. We're going to think only about that long, luscious summer we're going to spend at the beach—just you, me, the kids, and the mosquitoes. First, though, I've got to live through giving and grading end-terms, and you have to get to the doctor and find out what's making you feel pregnant even though you're not."

Toward the middle of the month, Marcie visited the internist. His diagnosis: She was anemic and suffering from young mothers' fatigue.

"What's the remedy?" Robert asked.

"Well, if the kids get stubborn and refuse to turn twenty-one overnight, I'm to take iron and vitamins and get plenty of TLC."

"I like the last part best."

"I thought you would—that's why I put it in. It's my own home remedy."

"Sounds like a sure cure to me. When can we test it?"

"How about half-past the kids' bedtime?"

For the remainder of the month, the remedies—both medical and home—worked so well that in June they almost forgot to pack Marcie's vitamins and iron pills along with her art supplies when they loaded up their rented car and headed for the cabin they had rented at the beach.

Chapter Three

Summer passed in a haze of brilliant sun and cooling ocean breezes. Inside the cabin, Robert wove his voluminous notes into the first draft of his Wharton biography; on the beach, Marcie set up her easel and created whimsical characters for Bambi Books as the children built sand castles at her feet.

There was time for everything in those sun-warmed days—for work and play and love. In the afternoon, their work put aside for the day, Robert and Marcie delighted in their children, the four of them picnicking, swimming, shell-hunting, and exploring as though they were the inventors of those joys. In the evening, their children sleeping off an overindulgence in sand and sun, they delighted in each other, walking hand-in-hand along the moon-lit beach, taking midnight swims, and lying in each other's arms beneath the stars.

As August wound down toward September, though, Marcie began to pale beneath her tan. She tired easily, had difficulty holding down her food, and began to suffer from the headaches she'd experienced before.

A week before they had intended, they closed up the cabin and returned home. The early return proved unnecessary; Daniel Halpern, their internist, was on vacation and would not be back until after Labor Day. An appointment was made for the first day the doctor would be available—the day Robert was due back for the fall semester at Seward College.

In the interim, Robert prepared for his classes and worked on the vita he'd have to submit to all the committees holding tenure hearings. Marcie took care of the children and worked on her illustrations. Both of them tried not to look worried.

At first, Robert was relieved when Marcie returned from her checkup to tell him that the doctor still could find no obvious cause for her symptoms. The relief shrivelled into a hard, cold lump in his chest, however, when she announced that the doctor was making arrangements for her to check into a hospital for tests.

"Tests?" He said it slowly, as though it were a foreign word he was pronouncing for the first time. "What kinds of tests?"

Marcie shrugged. "All kinds. He wants me to check in Sunday."

The cold lump in his chest constricted. "So soon?"

"That's what I said. I told him I don't feel *that* sick, but he says that the sooner he finds the cause, the sooner he can cure it."

"He has no idea what it is?"

"He seems partial to anemia or an out-of-whack metabolism, but we'll know for sure next week."

On Sunday afternoon, Sarah Resnick, Marcie's mother, arrived from the Bronx to take care of the children while Marcie was in the hospital. A tall, well-proportioned woman, Sarah looked closer to fifty than to her actual age of sixty-two. Her hair and eyes were dark like her daughter's. Her hair was peppered with gray now, though, and her eyes held less mischief than Marcie's—perhaps because they had seen more sorrow. She'd nursed Benjamin, Marcie's father, through a long, grueling, losing battle with cancer. The disease had been diagnosed when Marcie was twelve, and in the following four years there had been one operation after another, each one leaving Benjamin more of an invalid than the one that preceded it. The year Marcie was sixteen, the disease had finally drained the last dregs of his life during six long weeks when he lay in a coma in a sterile hospital room. The disease had exhausted more than Benjamin's life; it had drained all the family finances as well, forcing Sarah to become the family breadwinner, a role she was ill prepared for. Weekdays, she had worked as a clerk in a mail-order house, processing orders for vitamins and cosmetics until her eyes smarted and her fingers were numb. Monday and Thursday evenings and all day Saturdays, she worked as a part-time saleswoman in a midtown department store, her feet aching from the strain and her head whirling from the demands of pushing, shoving bargain hunters. She carried her burdens with a willing and loving heart, but she was determined that her daughters would be better prepared than she had been to catch any curves life might throw them; they would both have the college education she lacked. She saw Judith, her older daughter, through college, and Judith was now a teacher living in San Francisco with her lawyer husband and three children. Not until Marcie married Robert during her last year of college did Sarah give up her part-time job at the department store. She continued at her mail-order job, where she had worked her way up to head clerk, until her sixty-second birthday, when she embarked upon a well-earned early retirement. Now she enjoyed her independent life of leisure. She always had time for Marcie and Robert and her grandchildren when she was needed, but she had her own life and never interfered with theirs or overstayed her welcome. As a result, they had a loving relationship that grew warmer with each passing year.

The Sunday Marcie was to enter the hospital, Sarah arrived in time to have lunch with her and Robert. Throughout the meal, Sarah kept a casual, lighthearted conversation going, but Robert noticed that her hands were shaking a little.

After lunch, when Marcie went into the bedroom to gather some last-minute things, Sarah drew Robert aside.

"What are these tests really about?" she asked.

"Just what we told you, Ma. The doctor wants to check a few things out, that's all. He says he's sure it's nothing serious."

Her eyes got a faraway look, and Robert had the feeling that she was remembering the nightmarish times she'd lived through with her husband many years before. She turned her gaze back on him, studying his face.

"You're sure?"

For a moment his own unspoken fears rose up in him, but he pushed them down and managed a smile. "I wouldn't put you on, Ma."

The tension drained from her face, and she smiled too. She was still smiling when Marcie and Robert started out the door. She even managed to laugh when Marcie made a joke about not being able to resist a chance to have breakfast in bed. But as she kissed Marcie good-bye, Robert saw that some of the fear had crept back into her eyes and he hoped that Marcie didn't notice it too.

If Marcie had noticed it, she didn't mention it to him. She was in her usual good spirits during the taxi ride to the hospital, and she managed to hang on to those good spirits even while the reams of office red tape were being filled out.

Once she'd been properly admitted, Robert was allowed to see her to her room, where the floor nurse directed her to put on her pajamas. While she was in the bathroom changing, Robert chatted with two of her three roommates—a woman of about fifty, who was recovering from a gall-bladder operation, and one in her sixties, who was too busy complaining about the hospital meals and services to be specific about her own ailment. The third, an elderly woman of indecipherable age, slept, an intravenous in her arm.

Marcie emerged from the bathroom in the pajamas and robe she had bought for the occasion. "They don't waste time making you feel like an invalid, do they?" she said. She introduced herself to her roommates, then hopped up on her bed, sitting cross-legged, Indian style.

Robert pulled a chair over, and they sat for a while in silence, holding hands.

"Don't look so glum," Marcie said finally, her fingers tightening around his. "You know Dr. Halpern doesn't seem to think it's anything serious. He just wants to nail it down. He'll probably discover it's all in my head."

Robert smiled. "Well, if you need sessions on a couch to cure you, I'll be glad to volunteer."

A laboratory technician came in for a blood sample.

"Well, here we go!" Marcie said, rolling up her sleeve.

When the technician left, Marcie reached for Robert's hand again. "I think you should get back to the children. We should keep things looking like business as usual as much as possible."

He brushed her hair back from her face and gave her a tender kiss. "See you tonight."

He turned in the doorway to wave.

She was still sitting cross-legged on the bed. "If you see the Good Humor man, get the kids pops. Rachel likes chocolate chip and Benjie's partial to X-5 Jetstars."

Marcie kept up her high spirits throughout two long days of tests, but it was clear to Robert by Tuesday evening that her smiles and jokes were taking an effort.

"Well," she said when he came in that evening, "it looks like I won't be going home tomorrow after all. I thought I'd been pricked and probed and X-rayed in every possible place, but Dr. Halpern wants a few more tests, and a couple of his friends are to look me over tomorrow. So I get at least another day of breakfast in bed—and lunch, and supper."

"I'm going to have to talk to Halpern about that. He'll spoil you rotten." Robert tried to match her light tone, but his heart sank a little. With all that goddam modern equipment they had, why hadn't they found the trouble yet? He intended to call Halpern the next day and ask him to stop dragging his feet.

When he called the doctor's office the next morning, however, Halpern was unavailable; he was at the hospital making his rounds.

Sticking more needles into Marcie, Robert

thought, telling the answering service that there was no message, that he'd call back later.

When his morning classes were over and he returned to his office, he found a message from Halpern awaiting him. He dialed the doctor's office.

Halpern, the doctor's nurse told him, was with a patient at the moment, but he had told her to ask Dr. Silver to come to his office at four that afternoon to discuss his wife's condition.

"Can't he tell me over the phone?" Robert asked, not because he didn't want to go to the doctor's office, but because he sensed that news that could be related over the telephone would be less serious than news that must be delivered in person at a specified time.

"I'm sorry, but that's the only message the doctor gave me—to ask you to come in at four when his office hours will be over for the day."

"Look, I can cancel my afternoon classes and be there in less than an hour."

"I'm sorry, but the doctor said—"

"Yes, I know," Robert said. "Four o'clock." When he hung up, he noticed that the telephone receiver was wet with his perspiration.

He delivered his afternoon lectures like a computer programmed for teaching. He realized that the students weren't responding, but he wouldn't allow himself to think about it. Somehow, he sensed that if he thought about the students, he'd start thinking about other things too—like why Halpern insisted upon seeing him rather than speaking to him over the phone. So he concentrated on cold facts, automatic answers, and pat analyses until three o'clock, at which time he dismissed his last class a half-hour early.

"Oh, Bob!" Roscoe Bradcliff called after him in the hall. "I've been meaning to speak to you about your vita."

The last thing Robert wanted to think about at that moment was his tenure hearings, but he forced himself to turn and face the new chairman of his department.

Bradcliff fingered his wide, flowered tie. "Don't you think the vita would be more impressive if you added a few more published works to it?"

"I was going to tack on Leon Edel's *Henry James*, but I didn't think he'd go for that, so I decided to settle for my own meager list of published papers."

"It's not very much. What about the Beerbohm piece you told me you were working on?"

"He seems to be out of fashion at the moment. I've had two rejections so far. Right now, I'm waiting to hear from the *Midwestern Literary Quarterly*."

"Tough luck!" Bradcliff said, unable to hide the glee with which he always reacted to news of a colleague's failure. "You should have shown it to me first. I'd have been glad to give you a few pointers."

On rendering it unsuitable for publication, Robert thought. It was no secret that professional jealousy prompted Bradcliff to offer booby-trap advice to any colleague foolhardy enough to seek it. "I didn't want to intrude on your busy schedule."

"Nonsense! I'd have been happy to help. Of course, I've been up to my ears in the anthology I'm trying to get out on Chidiock Tichbourne."

"Tichbourne? I thought he wrote only one poem."

"That's what makes it so difficult—so difficult." He emitted a deep sigh. Whether it was evoked by his own troubles with the unproductive Tichbourne or Robert's forthcoming difficulties in tenure hearings was unclear. It was such a well-rendered sigh, however, that it might easily have covered both. "I wish *you* had been more productive. I don't know what to tell those committees when they ask me about the fact that you have only five published papers and one unpublished book listed."

"You might try saying I teach well."

"That's not what they're looking for."

"The more the pity."

Professor Tilman passed them. Bradcliff's eyes hardened as he returned Tilman's nod. They were still icy when he turned them back on Robert. "Well, let me know if you get any word on that Beerbohm piece. In the meantime, I'll do my best."

To screw me, Robert thought. "You don't know how much I appreciate that," he said, and he hurried out of the building.

He took a taxi to Halpern's office, arriving there at a quarter to four. Officially, Halpern's office hours ended at three, but there were still two patients in the waiting room, a middle-aged woman and a man with his arm in a sling.

After announcing himself to the nurse, he took a seat and extracted a paperback from his pocket. A great admirer of Joseph Conrad, he was rereading *Victory*, but he couldn't bring himself to concentrate on the lushness of the prose and the sensation of darkness and evil it evoked. He closed the book and reached for one of the magazines that were piled on a nearby table, wondering why doctors were so scrupulous about providing reading matter for their patients and so frugal about providing the light by which to read it.

A patient emerged from the inner recesses of the doctor's examining and consultation rooms. The nurse ushered the woman in to take his place.

Unseeing, Robert turned the pages of the magazine he held until he reached the end. He exchanged it for another and began the process all over again.

Three magazines later, the woman emerged, and the man with the sling was shown inside.

Returning to the waiting room, the nurse began straightening magazines and clearing her desk. Robert watched her as though every gesture she made was extremely important. It was; while he concentrated on her end-of-day activity, he didn't have to think about anything else. If she was aware that Robert was watching her, she gave no indication. She kept working, never allowing her eyes to meet his. Somehow that was more frightening than a brief glance of indignation or indifference might have been. Despite his determination not to think, the cold thought kept seeping in from the back of Robert's mind, like a draught that finds its way beneath closed doors: *Why won't she look at me?*

The man with the sling emerged, paused at the desk to make another appointment, and left. The nurse went into the doctor's consultation room, remained there for a few moments, and returned.

"The doctor will see you now." Her smile was cheerfully professional, but her eyes still did not meet his.

Taking heart from her tone—she wouldn't have sounded so cheerful if the news was really bad, would she?—Robert pulled himself to his feet and walked the thirty paces to the consultation room.

David Halpern was seated behind a huge mahogany desk in a room whose oak-panelled walls bore sufficient diplomas, certificates, and citations to impress even the most jaded of patients. A tall, well-built man in his mid-fifties, his dark hair graying gracefully at the temples, he always reminded Robert of the doctors who graced the pages of the *Saturday Evening Post* when he was a kid, rendering testimony that more of them smoked Kents than any other cigarette.

Rising as Robert entered the room, Halpern extended a hand across his desk. His grip was firm and sure. "Sorry you had to wait," he said, "but I thought it would be best if we saw each other when the patients were gone and we had time to talk without interruption."

Robert nodded and took the seat across from him. "I take it you've finished testing my wife."

Halpern reseated himself in his high-backed leather chair. "Actually, I was finished testing a while ago. What I've been doing is retesting and having consultations."

Robert's hands grew cold and damp. "That doesn't sound very good."

"It isn't." Halpern leaned forward, his face grave. "There's really no way I can put it that will soften it: Your wife is suffering from a highly malignant and inoperable tumor of the brain—spongioblastoma."

The sounds hit Robert's ears and bounced off again like foreign, incomprehensible words. He shook his head, trying to clear it, but he couldn't. "I'm sorry," he said. "I don't think I heard—I don't think I understand."

Halpern nodded and waited, giving him a moment to pull himself together. It didn't help. His brain still felt like a disaster area. His entire body had gone cold and numb, and his hands began to tremble.

Finally, Halpern reached for a book on his desk, riffled through its pages, and opened it to a drawing of the human brain, its parts neatly shaded and labelled. It was the type of drawing Marcie did for the medical and pharmaceutical pamphlets she sometimes illustrated.

Positioning the book on his desk so that they could both see it, Halpern extracted a gold pen from his breast pocket and pointed it toward the center of the illustration.

"This is the medulla," he said. "It's the most primitive part of the brain, controlling the heart, breathing, blood pressure. That's where the tumor is located."

"But can't you take it out—shrink it—do something?"

Halpern shook his head. "We can't operate on this part of the brain, and we can't use radiation. In the first place, the tumor is too widespread for radiation to help, and in the second, to reach the tumor, radiation would destroy so much other tissue that it would hasten her end, not prolong her life."

An incessant buzzing had started in Robert's head; he had to push his next words through it. "How much time—how much longer—" His voice broke.

"It's doubtful that she'll have more than six months. In the meantime, I can treat some of the symptoms, give her drugs that will ease the pain, help the nausea, make her comfortable—"

The buzzing crescendoed until Robert's brain seemed to explode. He jumped from his chair. "Comfortable! Goddam it! I don't want you to make her comfortable! I want you to make her live! What the hell good are all these goddam diplomas on your walls if you can't cure someone like Marcie?"

Halpern's jaw tightened. "I sometimes wonder myself."

Robert reached over and slammed shut the book that lay on Halpern's desk. "If you think I'm going to sit back and take your word as the gospel truth about her case, you're crazy! I'll take my wife to—"

"Dr. Silver!" His voice was calm but firm enough to halt Robert's tirade. "I have no objection to your seeking other opinions. I'll only point out that if you want the best men to look at your wife, you'll wind up right back where you started. Because the two top neurosurgeons in the city happen to be personal friends of mine and, at my request, they examined your wife and went over her test results today and gave me the same diagnosis I just reported to you."

Robert teetered a second, as though he'd been punched, then slumped back into his chair. "I'm sorry," he said, defeated. "I shouldn't have come down on you like that."

"Forget it. It's a perfectly normal reaction. You needed to hit back at someone, and I was available."

The ache behind Robert's eyes was almost unbearable. He pushed his glasses up and pressed his fingers against his eyelids.

"Can I get you something? I can give you a tranquillizer or a shot of whiskey."

He shook his head without raising it. "No. Just give me a minute."

For a while, the only sound in the room was Robert's jagged breathing.

Finally, he slipped his glasses back into place

and looked across at the doctor. "How long did you say?"

"Six—seven months at the outside."

"Pain. Will she have much pain?"

"It's hard to say. Everyone reacts differently. There will be the symptoms she has now—headaches, nausea, dizziness. We can give her something for that. She'll probably tire easily too. Later there may be other symptoms, from memory lapses to delusions to outright changes in personality. It's impossible to predict exactly how this type of tumor will affect a patient. Some have all those symptoms—even hallucinations and psychoses—others only a few."

"Oh, God!" The words were half prayer, half curse. "And the end?" He almost gagged on the word.

"She'll go into a coma."

"For how long?"

The doctor shrugged.

Robert buried his face in his hands. *Six months —seven at the outside.* . . . The doctor's death sentence kept reechoing in his brain. How could he face it? How could Marcie face it? But why *should* Marcie have to face it? Why should her last weeks and months of life be clouded by the fact that they *were* her last weeks and months? She was so full of the joy of living. Would it be fair to rob her of that and offer her a substitute of depression and despair?

"I told you today"—Halpern's voice cut through his thoughts—"to give you a chance to get over the initial shock, so you'll be strong enough to help your wife tomorrow when I tell her."

Robert's head shot up. "Tell her? My God! You can't do that!"

"But she must be told. It's her body, her life. She's an intelligent young woman. She'd want to know."

"Why? So that the last days of her life can be filled with the agony of knowing that she'll have to leave it before it's half begun, before she's had a chance to fulfill her dreams and to see her children grow up?"

"But there are things she'll want to do."

Robert leaned forward, pressing his hands on the desk. "No! Listen to me! There are things *I* wanted to do—*for* Marcie—things I've always dreamed of doing for her, giving to her. Now there'll never be time. But I can give her this—her last days without tears. I won't let you rob her of that."

"What you're asking me to do is to conspire with you to rob her of her right to know the truth about her condition." There was an edge on Halpern's voice.

"What I'm asking you to do is to ensure her right to peace of mind," Robert insisted.

"Are you sure?" Halpern asked, his eyes studying Robert's face, his voice softening a bit. "Are you sure it's her peace of mind you want protected —or your own?"

"What the hell does that mean?"

"It means that by denying your wife the right to

know she's dying, you may be trying to hide from that knowledge yourself."

Robert's face flushed with anger. "That has to be the stupidest, most twisted piece of amateur psychology I've ever had thrown at me. After all that has been said here, do you honestly think I can walk out of this room and repress the fact that my wife is dying?"

"You don't understand—"

"No, doctor. *You* don't understand. You don't understand me and you don't understand Marcie."

"And have you tried to understand me and my responsibility as your wife's doctor to tell her the truth?"

"Your responsibility as my wife's doctor ends where my responsibility as her husband begins. You're responsible for diagnosing and prescribing for her body. I'm responsible for everything else."

"You're taking on a great, unnecessary burden of responsibility by not telling her," Halpern said.

"Let me worry about that."

Halpern shook his head. "I still think—"

"Doctor, I don't give a damn what you think. You're not involved. It's what I know about my wife—what I feel for her—that counts. You're not to tell her the truth about her condition. There's nothing more to say about the matter."

"There's a great deal more to say. What about the symptoms she'll continue to have, the pain that's to come? What do you propose I tell her? She's far too intelligent to buy a simple there's-nothing-really-wrong-with-you after all the tests we've put her through and all the doctors who have poked around her."

"I'm sure you'll think of some adequate explanation for her symptoms. You can't tell me that you haven't done that with other patients before."

Halpern sighed. "No. And I can't tell you that I haven't usually regretted it too."

Robert's voice thickened. "Your regrets, Doctor, are nothing compared to mine." He got to his feet a little unsteadily. "There was so much I wanted to give her. And all it will come down to is a few short months of status quo."

Halpern rose also. "My car's outside. I'll drive you home."

"No, thanks. I need the walk."

He nodded and started toward the door.

"Dr. Silver."

His hand on the knob, Robert turned.

Halpern was still standing at his desk. In the late-afternoon light filtering through the window, his face looked more lined, more tired than before. "I'm sorry. Very sorry."

"Yeah. Me too." He closed the door softly behind him.

The reception room was dim and desolate. The nurse had left for the day, leaving only one lamp still burning. Robert glanced around as he walked through, nagged by the feeling he'd left something behind. But it was only the vague, elusive hope that dances attendance upon unenlightenment that he had lost—nothing that could ever be retrieved.

On the street, he paused in front of the doctor's

building, a huge, elegant apartment house that faced Prospect Park and had been the upper-class Jews' answer in the Twenties to the gentlemen's agreements that had kept them out of the side-street brownstones. For a moment, the wild idea of cutting through Prospect Park in the hope of being set upon and killed by muggers crossed his mind, but, with a shudder, he regained his senses and forced his footsteps toward Eastern Parkway and home.

Like an invalid who is learning to reuse atrophied muscles, he concentrated only on the mechanics of walking. Head bent, hands in his pockets, shoulders hunched, he watched his feet move as though they belonged to someone else. Right foot, left foot, right foot, left; it kept ominous thoughts at bay.

As he neared the large wrought-iron gates that marked the entrance to the Brooklyn Botanic Garden, his steps slowed, and, almost without conscious will, he found himself pushing through the turnstile and heading toward the long green called Cherry Lane. It was the one area of the park in which people were allowed to sit on the grass, and Marcie, like the other neighborhood mothers, often brought the children there.

It was now close to five o'clock, and only slivers of the late-afternoon sun slipped through the long shadows cast by the cherry and maple trees that bordered the long, lush green. Most of the mothers and children had long since departed to begin the early-evening rituals of bathing babies and preparing dinners, but there were a few stragglers—young women clad in dungarees and sweat shirts, picking up toys and calling to toddlers who peeked out from behind trees, then ran across the grass with shrieks of delight.

Robert sat down on the cool, damp grass, leaning his back against the trunk of one of the cherry trees. He looked up at its branches. Some of the leaves were changing color already, taking on delicate hues of yellow and pink. Soon they'd be falling to the ground. He thought of how Rachel and Benjie loved running through the leaves, collecting the colorful ones, jumping on the dried ones, delighting in the crisp, crackling sound. They enjoyed it almost, but not quite, as much as they enjoyed the cherry blossoms in the spring. He and Marcie were always awed by the magnificent sight of the cherries in all their splendor, their outstretched branches sagging beneath their majestic burden of pink-and-white blossoms. For the children, however, the real joy of cherry-blossom time came later, when spring breezes brought the petals down from the trees like a magic pink blanket of snow. Then, yelping with glee, Benjie and Rachel would roll in the soft, fragrant petals, gathering armfuls to shower over Marcie and Robert as they lay on the grass watching their antics.

Robert remembered how Marcie had laughed last spring as the children had dumped a load of petals over them, then rushed off to gather more. The blossoms had clung to her hair like a net jewelled with pink-hued pearls, and her eyes had sparkled with life and love and laughter. "Oh, God!" she'd joked. "I hope this isn't some crazy fertility rite. If it is, we're in trouble!"

Then, giggling, the children had returned to bury them under yet another load of blossoms.

To bury them.

To bury Marcie.

Oh, God! Robert closed his eyes and leaned his head back against the tree. *Oh, God!* He had to think. He had to think about what the doctor had told him. But his mind recoiled from the gaping hole that would be the future and tried to cover it over with visions of Marcie in the past: Marcie as she looked with cherry blossoms in her hair, contented and fulfilled; Marcie as she looked the first time he'd seen her and tried to pick her up, a smudge of charcoal on her cheek, her eyes filled with wariness—and mischief—and Marcie as she looked the day she married him, all radiance and love and desire.

He'd been so nervous on their wedding day—not because he feared marriage, but because he was afraid he could never measure up to be the kind of husband Marcie deserved. He remembered how awkward he had been when the rabbi handed him the goblet of wine from which they were both to drink—as they would thereafter share the cup of life. He'd had trouble managing Marcie's veil. Her eyes had met his, her lips puckering slightly to telegraph him an almost imperceptible kiss. Then she'd raised the veil herself and placed her warm, soft hand over his trembling one as he raised the silver cup to her lips. And with her touch, his trembling had fled.

Later, when the ceremony and the reception were over and they were in their hotel room in the Catskills at last, Marcie was the one who trembled. She tried to cover her nervousness by making jokes, unpacking her suitcase, inspecting their room, but he'd seen it there in the back of her eyes as her glance flitted over the bed and then away again. They'd had some pretty heavy necking sessions, but, of their own choice, they'd never made love; they had wanted their marriage to be a true beginning for them in all ways.

When Marcie slipped into the bathroom with her nightgown and negligee, he had quickly changed into his pajamas—the first pair he'd worn since he was a kid. She was a long time in coming out—long enough for him to work up a case of nerves too. He knew how crucial that night would be since Marcie was a virgin, but his own rather meager sexual experience left him far short of the finesse of a Casanova or Don Juan. He'd pored over marriage manuals during the last few weeks, but now their advice whirled in his brain like the indecipherable formulas of ancient alchemists.

Suddenly, the door opened, and Marcie stood there, her hair cascading over her shoulders, the light from behind outlining every contour of her body.

Robert gasped, his heart pounding, his thighs trembling. "Oh, God! You're beautiful!" he whispered. He longed to rush over and crush her to him, but he held back because she stood there like a butterfly poised for flight.

For a moment, they stood there, gazing at each other.

Let me be gentle, Robert thought. *Let me make the right first move.*

But it was Marcie who made the first move. Slipping off her negligee, she crossed the floor and stood in front of him, so close that the tips of her breasts touched his chest. Then she wound her arms around his neck. "I love you," she whispered.

He was able to take it from there.

He had thought on that day, nine years before, when Marcie had steadied his hand beneath the wedding canopy and put him at ease beside their marriage bed that he could never love her more. He had been wrong. There had been a good deal of adjusting and growing up to do those first few years, but they'd done it together, and as they had, he'd discovered that his love for the remarkable woman who had chosen to share life with him had grown too. It had continued to grow, through the bad times and the good, through the birth of their daughter and the birth of their son, through every passing day—until he had come to realize that the love he and Marcie shared was as infinite and as ever-expanding as the universe, the one constant in an ever-changing and chaotic world. Marcie had brought him more than love and friendship and understanding—she had brought him meaning. Without her—

His thoughts broke off as he sensed a presence

near him. Opening his eyes, he looked up into the craggy face of a guard.

"Park's closing in ten minutes, mister."

Nodding, he pulled himself to his feet and hurried to the side exit that was closest to home.

Rachel and Benjie hurled themselves at him in their usual enthusiastic welcome when he walked through the door. He held them tight, burying his face in first one neck and then the other.

"Your beard tickles!" Rachel giggled, pulling away.

"And you're hugging too tight!" Benjie complained.

In a second, they had both slipped from his arms and darted back to their TV program.

With a sigh, he straightened up and walked into the kitchen, where his mother-in-law was busy at the stove.

He planted a quick kiss on her cheek. "Hi, Ma."

"Hello, dear." Sarah returned the kiss. "Dinner's ready. I thought you'd be home a little earlier." It was a question, not a reprimand.

"I got tied up at school. I should have called. Sorry."

"Don't be silly. No harm done. You said you were going to call the doctor today. . . ."

He looked into her expectant face, saw the lines etched by both smiles and sadness. Marcie would look like that in thirty years. And then he remembered: Marcie wouldn't be here in thirty years; she wouldn't be here in ten, nor even in one. He turned quickly away, pretending he wanted to snitch some lettuce from the salad bowl.

"Oh, yeah. He thinks he's on the track of something. He'll let us know soon."

"Does he think it's serious?"

"No, no! Not from the way he talked." He swiped another piece of lettuce. "Say, what kind of dressing did you whip up for this? It's great!"

"Kraft's finest—and you know it." She slipped in front of him so that he'd have to look at her. "You're upset about something, Robert. I can tell. Is there something you're not telling me? You know, Marcie's father . . ."

He knew about Marcie's father—how he died a long and horrible death from cancer when Marcie was sixteen. He forced himself to look into Sarah's eyes. "No, Ma, really. If I'm uptight, it's because the department chairman at school has been giving me a hassle, but it's nothing I can't handle." He put his hands on her shoulders. "There's nothing seriously wrong with Marcie. Believe me."

He felt her shoulders relax beneath his grip. "Thank God!" she said. She turned away, but not before he saw her quick tears of relief. "Go help the children wash their hands. I'll get dinner on the table."

When Robert arrived for visiting hours that evening, Marcie was sitting cross-legged on her hospital bed, doing a crossword puzzle. She had braided her hair, and when she looked up at him, the two long plaits falling across her shoulders, she looked small and vulnerable, like their Rachel. That one glance was all that was necessary to reassure him that his decision in Halpern's office had been right: She deserved a cloudless end.

He raised his hand in an Indian salute. "How."

She looked down at her puzzle and made a face. "It won't fit. You'll have to do better." She reached up and pulled him down for a kiss. "*That's* better."

"I've always been a man of action."

"That's good because I've got plenty of action planned for you tomorrow morning."

"Like?"

"Like getting the hell over here the minute the cashier opens downstairs, paying my phone bill, and taking me home."

"I'm beginning to like that man-of-action image more and more. Do you know something I don't know?"

She nodded, her face glowing with happiness and relief. "Dr. Halpern was here a little while ago. He's going to let me flee the coop."

Robert felt as though his heart were slowing down, beating on tiptoe. "What did he say?"

"It's all very complicated, but, thank God, not very serious." She slipped off the bed and tucked her hand into his. "Come on. Let's go to the lounge, and I'll tell you."

The small visitors' lounge was crowded to overflowing, so they paced the long hospital corridor instead. As they walked, she filled him in on Halpern's diagnosis: She was suffering from anemia and also from a rare virus—one that had only recently been isolated, and that the doctors knew little about.

"They do know that it's recurrent—rather like malaria—and it's not contagious or even serious. They can't cure it, but they can treat the symptoms. The sieges usually last for months, but the remissions can go on for years." She shrugged. "Leave it to me to get something rare."

"You're a rare bird."

"As long as I'm not a turkey."

They paused at the end of the corridor in front of a window that looked down on dirty sidewalks and crumbling tenements. They stood there, holding hands, watching the wind swirl the litter in circles on the street.

"I've missed the kids so," Marcie said. "Talking to them on the phone is no substitute. It will be so good to get home."

"It will be so good to have you back home."

She turned and looked at him, her eyes glistening. "Oh, Bob! You'll never know how scared I was there for a while."

"I think I do know. I wasn't exactly feeling like a man of steel myself."

As they often did, his glasses had slid part way down his nose. Smiling, Marcie reached over, gently pushing them into place with her finger. "Thank God, it's all behind us now!" she said, slipping her arms around him.

He held her close.

"Right?" she asked.

He closed his aching eyes and rubbed his bearded cheek against her soft, smooth one. "Right," he said.

Chapter Four

The High Holy Days came late that year, falling in the golden early days of October when the sun still clings to its summer brightness but the air tingles in anticipation of fall. The same cocoon of numbness in which Robert protected himself after Marcie's return from the hospital fortified him through the Rosh Hashanah services at their temple. It kept him from flinching as the piercing sound of the shofar ushered in a new year whose end his Marcie would not live to see. It kept him from faltering as he prayed with Jews the world over that he and his family would be written in the Book of Life so that they might have yet another chance to prove themselves worthy of God's covenant by living in accord with His laws and His commandments. It kept him from averting his eyes as he exchanged *gut yontifs* with his neighbors and his friends.

But on Yom Kippur, that most awesome day of the year when a Jew must open his soul to his own scrutiny and to God's, the cocoon began to unwind. Slowly, like a postoperative patient coming out of anesthesia, Robert became more and more conscious of his pain.

It began on Yom Kippur Eve as he watched Marcie kindle and bless the holiday candles, her eyes reflecting their glow as she thanked God for His blessing of light. It intensified that evening in the synagogue through the haunting chant of the Kol Nidre, and swelled through the twenty-four-hour fast until it crescendoed in a piercing stab of pain as he stood beside Marcie for the memorial services at the end of the day. For, suddenly, the awful realization came: *Next year, I'll be saying* yizkor *for my wife.*

Sweat broke out on his forehead, and he began to tremble.

"Are you all right?" Marcie whispered, taking his hand.

He nodded. "Too much fasting, that's all."

"Do you want to sit down?"

He shook his head, taking a breath, willing his voice to be steady as he repeated the mourner's kaddish with the rest of the congregation: "*Yis-gad-dal v'yis-kad-dash sh'meh rab-bo. . . .*"

Finally, the prayer approached its conclusion.

"The departed whom we now remember have

entered into the peace of life eternal," the rabbi said, his white robe becoming a blur to Robert. "They still live on earth in the acts of goodness they performed and in the hearts of those who cherish their memory. May the beauty of their life abide among us as a loving benediction."

"Amen," the congregation answered.

"May the Father of peace send peace to all who mourn, and comfort all the bereaved among us."

"Amen," the congregants said and resumed their seats.

Robert was aware of Marcie's eyes on him as the choir sang the hymn that ushered in the concluding services.

"Do you want to leave?" she whispered.

"I'm fine," he insisted.

By the time the shofar had sounded its last piercing cry, Robert had himself under outward control. He was able to stand calmly beside Marcie for the benediction, his hand warm and steady as it sought hers. He managed not to flinch as the rabbi's prayer for a year he knew they could not see through together was offered up to God, interspersed with the choir's amens.

"And now, at the close of this day's service, we implore Thee, O Lord our God: Let the year upon which we have entered be for us, for Israel, and for all mankind: A year of blessing and of prosperity. A year of salvation and comfort. A year of peace and contentment, of joy and of spiritual welfare. A year of virtue and of fear of God. A year which finds the hearts of parents united with the hearts of the children. A year of pardon and favor. A year of peace.

"May the Lord bless thy going out and thy coming in from this time forth and forever. Amen."

Marcie turned to him. "Happy New Year, honey."

He kissed her, hoping she'd attribute the break in his voice to the rigor of his fast. "Happy New Year, sweetheart."

The numbness was gone. There was nothing left to cushion the brutal reality that lay ahead. In the days that followed, Robert felt like a snail that has been deprived of its shell: There was no place left for retreat.

At school, the pressure was on. At his tenure hearings before the personnel and budget committees and administration groups, Bradcliff's camp lined up against him, asking questions intended more to indicate their disdain than to glean information. He answered the questions, pretending he was unaware of their intent, refraining from telling the questioners to go to hell and to take the tenure they were dangling before him with them. A throbbing ache inside him kept reminding him that, for Benjie's and Rachel's sake, he'd need all the security he could get.

At home, he found it more and more difficult to meet Marcie's eyes, to speak to her of everyday things, to laugh and to love as before. Marcie was still waiting for the remission Halpern had promised her. The medication she was taking alleviated some of her symptoms, but not as much, Robert was sure, as she pretended it did. When they put the final touches on a membership brochure that he was writing and she was illustrating for their temple, he was aware of how often she closed her eyes tight then opened them wide, as if to clear her vision. When they had their meals, he observed the way she pushed the food around on her plate, eating slowly and methodically, as though she had to push every mouthful down—and keep it down by sheer force of will. And when they walked hand in hand as they had always done, he was conscious of a tightening of her grip, as though she needed her hand in his not only for affection but also for support. She tired more quickly too, and, though she never complained, the pain in her eyes bore witness to the fact that her headaches were getting worse.

Unable to bear the sight of her suffering—in the light of his knowledge of how it must end—Robert found himself trying to keep it from view. At first, he accepted any excuse to prolong his hours away from home; at last, he began making them up. He would invent committee meetings or substitute duty in evening-session classes, then spend the time thus bought walking the streets, nursing a drink in a lonely bar, or sitting in a movie theater, unaware of the action on the screen. But always, at the end of those evenings, there were Marcie and reality awaiting him at home. It was awkward when he returned while Marcie was still awake, waiting to ply him with curious, interested questions that had to be answered with lies.

Lately, she'd been awake more and more, her eyes heavy lidded as though she had to force them to stay open—but they watched him carefully as he tried to find plausible answers to questions that had become more and more probing. He began to feel something that he had never before known in his relationship with Marcie—guilt—and he tried to escape it by staying out even later and more often. He didn't know which was worse, returning home while Marcie was still awake and he had to dodge her questions, or returning home after she had gone to sleep, slipping into bed beside her, and lying there, watching the rise and fall of her bosom as he listened to her soft breathing, unable to forget for a moment it would soon be stilled.

He was grading papers in his office with the help of Betty Shapiro, his graduate-student assistant, late one afternoon at the end of November when Katherine Marish slipped up behind him.

"Honestly, Robert!" she pretended to scold, massaging his shoulders with her beautifully manicured hands. "You work too hard!" She turned her bright smile on Betty. "Betty, tell Dr. Silver that you're perfectly capable of doing this job alone. I'm going to kidnap him and make him buy me a drink."

Betty shrugged. "You've got the cart before the horse, Miss Marish. Dr. Silver doesn't need my permission to go, and, obviously, if he thought I was capable of doing the job myself, he wouldn't be here doing it with me."

Robert was startled at the note of sharpness mingled with hurt that he detected in Betty's voice. He liked her and respected her judgment; it never occurred to him that she might be misconstruing the long hours he had taken to working in his office as a lack of confidence in her ability. More to placate her than to humor Katherine, he pushed his chair back from his desk and reached for his coat.

"Hey, you know better than that!" he said. "I only stick around to see what I can learn from you."

"I have a few things I can teach you too," Katherine said with a slow smile.

Robert knew better than to turn one woman down in the presence of another, but he tried to set a casual limit. "Do you think you can sandwich them in over one drink? I'm due home soon." It was a lie—as was his earlier call to Marcie telling her that he was working late because he had a faculty meeting at eight.

"Well, I can make a start."

"I'm a fast learner," he promised, and, with a wave to Betty, he guided Katherine out of his office.

As they walked along Lexington Avenue to the "delightful little pub" Katherine recommended, it occurred to Robert that buying Katherine a drink was a good idea, even if it wasn't his own. She was a manipulator who played both ends against the middle, but she was fairly well entrenched with Bradcliff's clique. It wouldn't hurt to stay in her good graces. The question of her own tenure wouldn't be coming up until next term. In the meantime, she had the ears of the right people.

Perhaps he could strike a you-scratch-my-back bargain with her.

The pub was a combination of dim lights, mahogany panelling, and red-plastic upholstery. They took a back booth and ordered highballs. As they sipped their drinks, Katherine gossiped about their colleagues. With a few casual but well-placed questions, Robert learned that there was a slight schism in the Bradcliff camp over the question of his tenure: Professor Graystone thought he was cute, and one or two others were wavering because they sensed that his book might establish his reputation when it came out, thus making him a valuable person to know.

"Really, Robert," she said, "you should be more friendly."

Robert gave a noncommittal smile, wondering whether she meant he should be more friendly to the fence straddlers or to her.

She drained her glass. "We'll have another," she told their waitress, who was passing by.

Shrugging, Robert drained his glass too. He'd said one drink, but—what the hell? He was tired of drinking alone.

Over the next few drinks, their conversation wandered away from the college but stayed centered around Katherine. She told him her life history and her many accomplishments. Ordinarily, he found her egotism an annoyance and a bore, but now he found it relaxing to turn his thoughts away from his problems and to focus them on the life and the words of someone he didn't give a damn about.

By their fourth drink, Katherine had worked herself up to more recent times and the two years she had spent studying and traveling in England.

England.... He and Marcie had always dreamed of seeing England together. Now they never would....

Katherine paused in the middle of a sentence. "What's the matter, Robert? You look so pensive."

"Nothing." He shook his head, but his expression didn't change.

"I know what it is—you're hungry. Come on. My place is just a few blocks from here. I'll whip up the best spaghetti dinner you ever tasted."

Two sheets to the wind, he was feeling too sorry for himself to face being alone yet, but he knew better than to sail into Katherine's port. He got her to compromise on an Italian restaurant in the Village.

They had a bottle of Chianti and a long, leisurely dinner, followed by Irish coffee in a "darling" coffeehouse Katherine had discovered.

He took her to her door, but declined her offer of a nightcap.

"Next time," she said, running a slender figure along the edge of his beard.

Robert nodded noncommittally, pretending not to notice her upturned face and moist, parted lips.

Because it was well after midnight when he arrived home, he was surprised to find Marcie still up. She usually went to bed early, unable to fight off the heavy tiredness that was one of the symptoms of her condition. She was sitting on the sofa, though, fully dressed, her eyes red rimmed and unusually bright.

Robert's heart slowed down, but he tried to keep his voice casual as he bent to kiss her. "Hey, it's past your bedtime, Cinderella."

She turned her face away so that his lips missed hers and landed in the vicinity of her ear. "You smell like a distillery."

"You know how these faculty meetings are now that they've voted to sell liquor in the lounge."

"No, I don't know how they are. Tell me. What happened at this one?"

He slipped out of his overcoat, tossed it over one chair, and sank down on another. "There was about as much accomplished as ever—not a damn thing. There was the usual backbiting—"

Marcie jumped to her feet, her hands clenched. "For God's sake! Stop lying!" she cried. "You may have lost your love for me, but surely you haven't lost your respect for my intelligence."

Robert sank back in his chair. He had never sobered up so fast in his life. "What the hell are you talking about?"

"You know damn well what I'm talking about—your *faculty meeting*. It was attended by a grand total of two—you and Katherine Marish."

His heart sank, but he tried to bluff it out. "You're crazy!"

"Oh, am I? Then maybe you better fire Betty Shapiro because she's crazy too. I called your office around five to ask you to pick up some supplies for me at the student commissary. Betty answered and told me you'd just stepped out with Katherine for a drink and would be coming home soon." She took a breath, her eyes filling with tears. "I told her that you'd be returning to school instead because there was a faculty meeting on the agenda, and I asked her to leave a message on your desk. That's when she told me that there was no faculty meeting, that there hadn't been one scheduled in the evening for ages."

"What does she know about it?"

"Plenty—as a graduate student–teacher observer!"

He was tired and he'd drunk too much. He felt as though his brain was working in slow motion. Desperately, he prodded it to come up with some logical explanation. "By the time I realized I'd made a mistake about the meeting, Katherine was nagging me to buy her a drink. She's always after me about it. I thought it would be a good time to do it and get her off my back." It was the best he could come up with.

"Then why did you lie to me about it now?"

"Because I was afraid you wouldn't understand—and I was right!" He attempted an accusatory tone. "For God's sake, Marcie! Let's not make a whole *tsimmes* out of a couple of lousy drinks!"

"A *couple* of drinks!" Her voice rose. "Robert, I called your office at five o'clock. It's after midnight now. Where the hell did you drink them—in a motel?"

He jumped up from his chair. "That's a lousy thing to say!"

"It's a lousier thing to do!"

He rushed over and grabbed her shoulders. "You know me better than that!"

"No, I don't!" she cried, shaking his hands off. "I don't think I know you at all anymore. You tell me you have to attend faculty meetings—yet, there have been none. You tell me you have to work late—yet, I know your work load is no different than before. And those evening-session classes you say you've been substituting in—how can I be sure they even exist?"

"Because I say they do."

"Like you said the faculty meetings did? If I called Bradcliff right now and asked him about those classes, what would he say?"

"Do you trust me so little?"

"What would he say, Bob? Answer me! What would he say?"

Her face had gone as pale as one of her blank canvases, and her eyes glared out of it like two dark slashes of light. His heart sinking, Robert averted his gaze.

"Damn you! You've been with her every one of those nights, haven't you? Damn you, *damn you!*" Bursting into sobs, she slumped down on the sofa.

Every sob, every shake of her shoulders was like a kick in Robert's gut. He sank down beside her. "No, Marcie! That's not true. There was only to-night, and even that was nothing—just too many drinks and a lousy Italian dinner."

"And all those other nights—how do you explain them?"

He ran his hand over his face. How *did* he explain them? "I was just walking, that's all. And drinking sometimes. I've been going crazy with this tenure thing. I—I didn't want to bother you with it." It sounded weak and implausible to his own ears.

She looked up at him, her eyes brimming with tears. "Since when has that damn tenure meant so much to you? You always said that if it didn't come through, you'd pick yourself up and start over someplace else."

"I've changed my mind. I'm thirty-five years old. I don't want to throw away the last five years of my life and start over someplace else."

"And that's why you lied and stayed away from home?"

"Yes. I didn't want to bother you. I know you haven't been feeling so hot, and—"

Her eyes flashed. "*So hot!* What do you know about how I've been feeling? What do you know about living with pain and nausea every hour of the day? Do you know how it feels to have your vision suddenly blur or double, to have the ground turn to a roller coaster beneath your feet? If you really cared about how I felt, you would have told me about your problems, not tried to add to my troubles by having me agonize over why you were lying and sneaking away from me!"

"All right. Maybe I was wrong not to tell you

how worried I've been about this damn tenure business, but—"

"Shut up, will you? I can tell by your face that you don't believe a word you've been saying. You're not only a rotten, lousy husband, Bob—you're a rotten, lousy liar too."

"Marcie, listen to me. I love you. My God! I never thought I'd have to beg you to believe that! I—"

"Stop it!" She jumped away from the hand he reached out to her and ran over to the window, her back to him. "I don't know what I hate you for more—going to bed with that thinking man's Moll Flanders or still lying to me about it now that I know!"

"But there's nothing between us!"

"Right! Probably not even a nylon nightie. She looks like the type who sleeps in the raw."

"Will you listen to me?" His voice rose in frustration and desperation.

"No!" She whirled on him, her eyes blazing. "I'm through listening to you—to your tales of faculty meetings and night work, to your lies piled on lies. You're the worst kind of sneak there is, Robert—the kind of man who wants to hold on to two women. Well, she may not care if you have a wife on the side, but I'll be damned if I'll stand for a mistress on the side. If you want her so much, you can go to her!"

"I never went to her, and I don't intend to go to her now!"

She picked up his overcoat and hurled it at him. "Well, you're sure as hell not staying here!"

"Dammit! This is my home too. You can't throw me out!"

"Just try me! I—" She stopped abruptly, blinking her eyes as though to clear her vision. Pressing her clenched fists to her temples, she sank down on a chair.

"Your head!" Robert said, rushing over to her. "Can I get you something?"

She closed her eyes. Slowly, as though the movement was agonizing, she shook her head. "You can just get the hell out of here," she said. "Just go!"

He stood there a moment, his coat in his hand. He didn't want to leave her, but he was afraid that if he stayed, her fury would make her symptoms worse.

"Will you get out of here?" she cried.

"All right, but I'll be back tomorrow after work. We have to talk."

"There's nothing to talk about."

"There's nothing to yell about. There's plenty to talk about."

She turned her face away.

He slipped on his coat and walked down the hall to the children's room. Rachel and Benjie slept soundly in their beds, unaware of the emotional violence committed by their parents in the other room.

As usual, Benjie had wriggled to the foot of his bed. Robert lifted him tenderly, placing his head back on his pillow after removing a fire engine and a dump truck from beneath it. He kissed his cheek, brushing his hair back from his forehead.

Rachel slept uncovered, her nose buried in the belly of her Raggedy Ann. Robert loosened her grip on the doll so that she'd have more breathing space. He pulled the covers up over her shoulders and tucked them in. He lingered a moment after kissing her. Then he turned and left the room.

Marcie was still on the sofa, her head between her hands.

"Will you be all right?" he asked.

"I'll never be all right again," she said, "but the sooner you leave, the sooner I'll be able to make a stab at it."

"I'm going only because you're so upset. I'll be back tomorrow when you've had a chance to calm down."

She didn't answer.

He paused at the door. "I may have lied to you, Marcie, but I never cheated on you. I love you." Despite his effort to control it, his voice broke.

Her back was still turned to him when he left the apartment.

A November rain was falling when he went out into the street. He turned his collar up, but it was little protection against the icy needles the wind hurled in his face. He jammed his freezing hands into his pockets and lowered his head into the wind. His cheeks became numb, and his ears grew cold and red. His glasses fogged and his eyes began to sting, but that was more from his tears than from the elements.

He headed toward the subway, unsure where he should go. He was reluctant to turn to family or friends because it would mean giving explanations he was not prepared to make. In the station, he took out the address book he carried with him and began to leaf through it. The second time around, he stopped at *D*. He put a token in the turnstile and took the next train to Manhattan.

A half-hour later, he was standing with his finger pressed firmly against a doorbell.

"Who the hell is it?" a voice growled from behind the door.

"Robert Silver."

"Christ!"

The door swung open; Arthur Dowley stood barefoot in rumpled pajamas. "Trick or treat was a month ago. You picked a cockeyed time to catch up on it."

"I know this is *chutzpa* of the first order, but can you put me up for the night?"

He stood aside to let Robert in. "If you don't mind a lumpy sofa."

"Even the floor will do. I just want to get in out of the cold."

Dowley got a hanger and handed it to Robert. "That's what life is all about. Some of us never find anyone who'll open the door. Hang your coat in the bathroom. It looks soaked through."

When Robert returned from the bathroom, Dowley handed him a drink. He'd put on his glasses, but not his slippers.

"You want to talk about it?"

Robert shook his head.

They had their drinks in silence. Then Dowley went into another room and returned with a pillow and some blankets. He tossed them onto the couch.

"I have only one other pair of pajamas, and it's in the laundry. You'll have to sleep in your shorts or in the raw."

Robert nodded, slipped off his tie and began unbuttoning his shirt. "Dowley," he said to his host's retreating back.

Dowley turned, fixing his ever-present scowl on him.

"Thanks."

Dowley shrugged, but remained where he was instead of going on to his room. Finally, he said, "How the hell did you come to pick me?"

"Because I trust you. Because you don't ask questions or tell tales."

Dowley stood there, rubbing his hand over his unshaven cheek. "I don't give advice either, but once in a while I come up with an observation. Here's one: Some women are worth the hell they put us through." He turned and walked out of the room without another word, not even good night.

It was the longest night Robert had ever spent. Longer than the nights when Marcie was in the hospital and he had lain alone in their bed, oscillating between the height of hope and the peak of fear; longer than the nights he had lain beside her since her return, plunging through the murky depths of despair.

Over and over, he reviewed her outburst. Halpern had said she might become irrational, even paranoid. Could her accusations have been a symptom that her condition was entering that nightmarish phase? A chill that had nothing to do with his light covers and the draughty room ran through him. He couldn't—wouldn't—accept that. He examined his own behavior—his absences, his evasions—and realized that Marcie had every right to put her own interpretations on them. Only a child or a fool wouldn't have begun to suspect that something fishy was going on. Damn! How could he make things right between them again without telling her the truth?

He closed his eyes and pulled the blanket up around his shoulders, exposing his feet. He'd give her time to cool off. That had always worked in the past. A day apart, and they were always ready to discuss civilly and logically what they had been at each other's throats about the night before.

Tomorrow, he wouldn't even call her. He'd go to school and teach his full schedule of classes. By the time he went home, she'd be calm and reasonable again, ready to accept his explanation that it was his tenure hearings that had him so uptight.

But what if she still won't believe you? It was as if someone had asked the question aloud. The sound of it echoed in the room for the rest of the night.

Just before six, he drifted into a restless sleep.

There was no sign of Dowley when Robert awoke. He pulled on his trousers and walked barefoot into the kitchen. There was a place set for one at the table, a box of corn flakes and a jar of instant coffee in front of it, along with a note, scrawled across the back of an old envelope:

Have to get to an early class.
Help yourself to a bachelor's spartan breakfast.
Hope you won't need this tonight.
A. D.

Lifting the envelope, Robert discovered a key. *I hope to hell I won't too,* he thought.

The day was as long as the night had been. At three-thirty, when his last class ended, he shook off the stragglers who wanted to rehash points sufficiently covered in class and hurried to his office for his coat.

A message lay on his desk: "Call home."

Relief washed away all the hours of tension. It was better than he'd dared to hope: Marcie had made the first move.

He dialled the number quickly, tapping his fingers against his desk in happy impatience as he waited for an answer.

"Hello?"

His heart sank at the sound of his mother-in-law's voice. "Ma? Is Marcie there?"

Sarah's voice was hesitant. "Didn't you get my message?"

"Message?" He reread the note on his desk. "There was a message to call home. I thought it was from Marcie."

"It was from me." There was a pause. Then she asked, "Did Marcie call you at all today?"

"No. Ma, what's wrong?"

"Probably nothing." She was trying to sound cheerful. "It's just that Marcie called me early this morning and asked me to stay with the children for a while. I got over around nine, and she left, saying she had some research to do for one of those brochures she illustrates. She said she wouldn't be long." She forced a little laugh. "I guess I'm acting too much like a mother, but—well, she's always called me before when she was going to be late."

"She probably just lost track of the time, Ma. Don't worry about it. I'm leaving now, so I'll be home soon, but I bet Marcie will get there before I do." He hung up, hoping he had sounded more confident than he felt. Then he grabbed his coat, ran out of the college, and jumped into the first cab he could get. To keep from panicking, he tried to keep his mind blank all the way home.

As usual, as soon as he was in the door, Rachel and Benjie ran to greet him, but his heart sank when he saw Sarah standing behind them, slowly shaking her head.

The children ran back to whatever they'd been doing, and Robert followed Sarah out to the kitchen.

"Still no word?"

"No word."

He sank down on a chair. "Did she say where she was going?"

"No. Only that she was going to do some research for a brochure."

"Brochure? I thought she was concentrating on the Bambi deal. I didn't know she had a brochure in the works."

Sarah shrugged. "Well, that's what she told me, dear."

"Maybe she got an assignment she forgot to mention to me." He tried to sound casual, tried to ignore the warning bell that seemed to be ringing in the back of his mind. "At any rate, she must have gone to the library. That's where she does all her research. For all we know, she lost track of the time and is still there, poring over a pile of books. I'll give them a call."

It wasn't until he had located the library's number in the telephone book that Sarah spoke again, her eyes filled with the puzzle of a sudden memory.

"There was something strange," she said. "It's the first time I can remember her going off to do research and not taking her sketchbook with her."

The warning bell got louder as Robert reached for the wall phone over the kitchen table.

It took a few minutes for him to convince the operator to let him speak to the librarian in the stacks, but he finally got through to him.

"Hi," he said, trying for an offhanded, friendly tone. "My name is Silver. My wife's an artist, and she usually goes over to you to do research for the booklets she illustrates. Her name's Marcia Silver. Do you know her?"

"Sure, I know Mrs. Silver." The voice on the

other end was cheerful, helpful. "She was here today."

"Was? Oh. I thought she might still be there. She hasn't come home yet, and a, uh, small family emergency has come up. Are you sure she's gone?"

"Oh, yes. She was here most of the morning, but she left—oh, I'd say, around noon."

"You wouldn't happen to know what she was doing research on, would you? She might have gone someplace to follow it up."

"Well, I can't tell you offhand, but if you can hold on, I'll check through today's call slips and let you know."

Robert drummed his fingers on the table while he waited, pretending not to notice how anxious Sarah looked, hoping she wouldn't notice how anxious he felt.

The seconds dragged by. Finally, there was the sound of papers being rustled at the other end.

"Mr. Silver? I have the call slips, but I don't know how much help they'll be. They don't seem to be limited to one subject."

"Oh?" He held his breath.

"She had out several books. Some were on the brain and the nervous system, some were on diseases of the blood, and some were on cancer."

Robert felt as though someone had opened a valve and was letting all the blood rush out of his body.

"I don't know of any one place she might have gone to follow through on all those subjects." The librarian's voice was still cheerful, helpful. "If you like, I can check a list of foundations and organizations for you. Of course, offhand, there's the American Cancer Society and—"

"No, that's all right. Thanks. I think I know the place they probably led her to."

"Oh. Well, in that case—"

"Yes. Thanks very much. You've been very helpful."

"My pleasure."

"Robert! What's wrong? You're so pale!" Sarah cried as he hung up. "What did they say? Do you know where she went?"

"I'm not sure, Ma. I have to make one more phone call. His hand was trembling so much he had to dial the number twice.

"Dr. Halpern's office."

"This is Robert Silver. I have to speak to him."

After a pause, Halpern's voice came over the wire. "Yes, Dr. Silver?"

There was no time to waste on preliminaries. "Was my wife in to see you today?"

"Yes, she was. I suppose she told you—"

"Told me! She hasn't told me anything. She hasn't been heard from since about nine o'clock this morning. What the hell did *you* tell *her*?"

"Nothing she hadn't already figured out for herself. Now, see here, Dr. Silver," Halpern rushed on before Robert could get a word in, "I told you from the beginning that I was against hiding the truth from her. When she came to me with it herself, I decided that the time for lying was over. It was my decision to make. At that point, it had become strictly a doctor-patient matter, and there was no room for the wishes of any third party."

"All right. I understand that. But why the hell didn't you call me to come meet her?"

"I wanted to, but she wouldn't let me. She insisted she was all right and said she was going straight home. She seemed all right. I mean, it wasn't as if the news was a shock. She'd figured it out for herself."

"Goddam it! Why didn't you call me anyway?"

Halpern sighed. When he spoke again, his voice was tinged with weariness and regret. "I'm only a doctor, not God. I can't make all the right decisions."

"Yeah, okay. I'm sorry. I shouldn't be yelling at you, but I'm scared stiff. She hasn't been home since this morning. God only knows what she might do."

"She's a levelheaded, intelligent woman," Halpern reassured him. "She was in good condition when she left here. She probably just wanted some time alone. I'm sure she'll be home in a little while."

Robert hung up the phone and sat staring into space.

"*Now* will you tell me?" Sarah's soft voice cut into his thoughts.

They were still in the kitchen, seated at the table. He reached over and covered her hand with his.

"She's dying, Ma," he said.

For a moment, she sat there in silence, her eyes

glistening with tears. "I think—" she said finally, slowly, as though forcing the words past an obstruction in her throat, "I think I knew it all along. Only, I wanted so much to believe you." Her tears spilled over, and she buried her head in her arms.

Robert got up and stood silently behind her chair, gently touching her shoulder. He knew that he could no more comfort her than she him. After a while, he walked away, took a bottle of wine down from a shelf, and poured her a glass. He went back and stroked her hair.

"Come on, Ma. Come on," he coaxed gently. "Drink this."

She looked up finally and took the glass, making an effort to get herself under control. "Sit down," she said. "I'll be all right now."

He sat opposite her, and she took his hand.

"How terrible these past months must have been for you!"

"I've made a rotten mess of everything, Ma." He turned his face away so that she wouldn't see the tears crowding his eyes. "I didn't want her to know, and I couldn't stand knowing myself. I was a bastard. I made all sorts of excuses to stay away from home. She—she thought I was seeing someone. We had a terrific row about it last night." He turned back to her. What did it matter if she saw the tears in his eyes? He knew she could hear them in his voice. "Now she's figured out the truth about herself, but she still doesn't know the truth about me. My God, Ma! What if she's leaving me?"

Sarah stroked his hand, shaking her head. "She

loves you," she said. "I don't think she could leave you any more than you could leave her. She's a smart girl, my Marcia. Now that she realizes the truth about herself, she'll be able to work out the truth about you."

"I wish I could believe that."

"You'll see. She'll be back." She stood up. "But when she comes, I don't think you'll need anyone else underfoot—not me and not your children. I'll take Rachel and Benjie back to my place for the night."

"Are you sure you're up to it?"

"It will be good for me. I'll get their things together."

A short time later, Sarah was herding the excited children out the door.

"Grandma's going to let us make popcorn," Rachel reported, her eyes shining as she kissed Robert good-bye.

"And stay up till nine o'clock!" Benjie added.

Robert hugged them both. "Be good for her."

"They're always good for me."

"You know something?" Robert said, kissing her. "The next guy who makes a mother-in-law joke in front of me is going to walk away with a black eye."

An unearthly quiet seemed to hover over the apartment after Sarah left with the children. Robert wandered through the rooms, feeling like a stranger, realizing how seldom he was there alone. Only the thought of Marcie coming home to an empty apartment kept him from going out to search for her, though he had no idea where to look. He couldn't even conduct an armchair search from the telephone because he knew it would stir up a hornets' nest of questions from family and friends. Besides, for too long, he and Marcie had confided only in each other. Even if she still harbored her suspicions of the night before, she wouldn't know how to turn to anyone else.

He sank down on the sofa, his head between his hands. *Just let her come home soon. Just let her be all right.*

Every other minute, he looked at his watch, amazed to see that at least an hour had not passed since the last time he had checked.

He began to pace again. He picked up books, put them down. He looked out the window, opened the door, looked down the hall.

At 10 P.M., he called the police.

The officer he spoke to could offer him only sympathy, not help. It was much too soon to file a missing person's report. Men did this sort of thing all the time. Now, with women's lib, the girls were getting into the act.

"Not my wife!" Robert insisted.

"Well, sir, there's always a first time." He chuckled confidentially. "Let's face it, if you took off for a night on your own, you'd get pretty riled if your wife had every cop in the city out looking for you, wouldn't you?"

"But you don't understand! She found out some terrible news today. She—"

"All the more reason why she'd want some time

alone. Now, my advice to you is to have a couple of drinks and go to bed. When you wake up in the morning, she'll be there."

"But—"

"I'll tell you what: If she's not back by this time tomorrow night, you give us another call. Okay, fella?"

Robert slammed down the receiver and began pacing again.

At 11:32, he sank down on the sofa, burying his face in his hands in an agony of despair. That was when he heard the key in the lock. He was up like a shot, but Marcie was inside the door before he reached it.

He wanted to yell at her, to shake her, to lash out at her for the agony she'd put him through. And he wanted to take her in his arms and never let her go. Yet, one look at her and his body turned rigid, his words freezing in his throat. Her open coat hung loosely from her shoulders, her hair hung down in ragged, wind-blown tangles, and her dark eyes stared out from her pale face, looking vague and wild at the same time. She seemed to be looking through him rather than at him, and, his heart sinking, Robert wondered if she recognized him.

"Do you know what I did tonight?" she asked, her voice as vague as her eyes.

Robert shook his head, afraid that if he spoke or moved toward her, she'd take flight like a startled bird.

"I walked across the Brooklyn Bridge. Walt

Whitman has a poem about that, doesn't he? About walking across the Brooklyn Bridge?"

Slowly, still apparently only half aware of him, she drifted past Robert. He followed her into their living room, where she stood in a daze, looking around at their book-lined walls. "It's here somewhere."

"Marcie."

With a slow shrug, she turned away from the books. "It doesn't matter," she went on, as if Robert had not spoken. "I know I didn't see and feel the things he did. I didn't see anything except the blackness of the river. I didn't feel anything except the cold. Do you want to hear something funny?" She was still looking through him, not at him. "I went on that bridge with every intention of jumping off it. I wanted to commit suicide because I'd found out I was about to die, and I was afraid."

For the first time since she'd walked through the door, her eyes met his. The glaze slipped away, revealing the torment and the fear it had been screening. "You should be laughing," she said, trying to twist her trembling lips into a smile. "That should be the funniest thing you've ever heard—that your stupid wife wanted to commit suicide because she was afraid of dying!"

Robert shook his head, his eyes glistening. "I could never laugh at you," he said. "Not when I love you so much."

She bit her lip and closed her eyes. When she opened them, they were filled with tears. "Oh,

Bob!" she said, her voice trembling. "I love you so. I don't want to die—to leave you. Oh, God! I'm so scared!"

"Me too," he said.

And then the barrier was down, and they were crying in each other's arms. It was the first time Robert had given way to the flood of tears dammed up inside him, and his body shook with waves of raw, tormented sobs. He and Marcie clung to each other like drowning people clutching their last hope.

"Oh, Bob, Bob! Hold me close! Don't let me die!"

He forced his way up through his tears and back into control. It was his strength Marcie needed now, not his weakness. "Hush, darling, hush," he whispered, rubbing his wet cheek against hers. "I love you."

Gradually, her sobs waned to a whimper.

Gently, he slipped her coat from her shoulders, smoothed her hair back from her face, and led her to the sofa.

"I'm an awful coward, aren't I?"

He shook his head. "Everyone's afraid to die. Cowards are the ones who are afraid to live. I—" He tried to swallow back the lump in his throat. "I'm the coward. I don't see how I'll be able to live without you."

Her eyes filled with a different fear. "But you have to! For Benjie and for Rachel!"

"You know I will."

She nodded, and closed her eyes.

He took her hand. "We have to talk about last night. Marcie, you have to believe me. There's never been anything between me and Katherine."

"I know that." When she opened her eyes, there was no trace of last night's suspicions. "I think I knew it last night too, but I was half hoping I was right." She looked at Robert's startled face and shook her head sadly. "That's another big yak, isn't it?" She sighed. "It's really not as crazy as it sounds. At first, I was so desperate to live and be well that I was ready to swallow any story you and Halpern gave me. But as hard as I tried, I couldn't keep myself deaf, dumb, and blind forever. I began to have my doubts. They got worse whenever I'd catch you watching me when you thought I wasn't aware of it, and when you started making all kinds of excuses to stay away from home, they multiplied like rabbits."

The bitter taste of self-loathing welled up in the back of Robert's throat. "I was a first-class bastard. I never meant to hurt you."

"I know, I know." Her voice wás as soft as it was when she was soothing one of the children. She got up and walked over to the window. "It's just that when you did begin staying away, I realized that it could be for only one of two reasons: Either I was mortally sick, and you loved me too much to watch what was happening to me; or I wasn't seriously ill, and you'd found someone else."

"Marcie—"

"No, let me finish." She turned from the window and faced him. "Anyway, after I called your office yesterday, I realized I had to stop fence-sitting and find out which of those possibilities was the reality. I opted for the other woman because I knew I could fight her for you and win. I couldn't fight death." She drew a deep breath. "Deep down, though, I knew I was wrong. You've always loved me too much."

His eyes misting, Robert walked over to her. "You're wrong. I could never love you enough."

"You see?" she asked, just managing to curve her lips into a smile. "You love me too much to know you love me too much."

"Your hands are so cold," he said, taking them in his.

"Not as cold as all of me will be soon."

An icy sheet of dread slipped over him. "Don't talk about it," he begged.

"Don't you see that I have to talk about it? I have to talk about so many things. But not now. Now, it's still too new. Promise me, though, that you'll hear me out when I'm ready."

"And what about now?"

"For now, just make love to me. Hold me so close that we can both forget for a little while."

Hand in hand, they went into their room, where they made love with a tender desperation that left no room for the shadow of death to wedge itself between them.

Sarah arrived with the children the next morning in time for a second cup of coffee. Benjie and Rachel reported their adventures at Grandma's at length, leaving little opportunity for the grownups to talk. When they finally ran off to their room to play, Marcie apologized for the day before.

"You must have been awfully worried," she said. "I'm sorry, Mom."

"It's all right. Bob told me everything." Sarah reached across the table for her daughter's hand. "Oh, Marcie! Can you believe me when I say I wish with all my heart that it was me instead of you?"

Marcie looked into her mother's eyes. "I believe you, Mom," she said, her voice as tender and as loving as the look on her face. "I'm a mother too."

Quietly, Robert pushed back his chair and slipped out of the room, giving the two women a moment alone.

The week that followed was a difficult one. Robert had thought that the tension might ease now that Marcie knew the truth, but he found that all that had really changed was that his concern turned from his own sorrow to Marcie's as he was forced to stand by, helplessly watching her vacillate between bitterness and despair.

That Saturday night, they were scheduled to attend a dinner at their temple given by the trustees in honor of congregants who had furthered the work of the temple over the past year; apparently, their membership pamphlet qualified them for an invitation. In the morning, Marcie said she didn't want to go, but she was pensive all day, and, by evening, she had changed her mind.

Dressed in a red-velvet pants-suit that heightened her color, Marcie looked more like her old self than she had in a long time. As she laughed and joked with their table companions throughout the meal, Robert was almost able to pretend that it wasn't all an act, that he didn't notice the sadness in the depths of her eyes, that they were destined to live happily ever after.

After the speeches had been suffered through and coffee was being served, Jack Levine, a lawyer with literary leanings who was seated on Robert's left, cornered him in a one-way conversation about current trends in the theater. Robert wasn't exactly sure how long Marcie had been gone when he realized that she had slipped away from the table, but when ten minutes more passed and she hadn't returned, he began to fear that she had taken ill. He excused himself casually and went down to the floor where the temple offices and rest rooms were located. While he was waiting for an answer that did not come to his knock on the ladies' room door, he heard Marcie's voice coming from the rabbi's study. He knocked there too.

The door was opened by Rabbi Klein. "Ah, Robert," he said. "Come in. Your wife and I were just talking."

Marcie was sitting on a dark-leather sofa, looking more pale than before.

"I was worried about you. Do you feel okay?"

She nodded.

He hesitated a moment, but when she said nothing, he started toward the door. "I'll wait upstairs."

"Bob."

He turned.

She bit her lip. "You've been through enough. I didn't want to inflict this—this search of mine on you too, but I always feel so alone now. I'd like it if you stayed."

He sat down beside her, taking her hand.

The rabbi walked over and sat in a chair near them rather than behind his desk. Simon Klein was a scholarly man in his mid-fifties who looked more at home here among the books lining his study wall than he had looked upstairs among his partying congregants a short time before.

"Marcia just finished telling me about her condition, Robert," he said. "I can't tell you how sorry I am."

Robert knew the man was sincere, but he couldn't help challenging him. "That's not much comfort from a man of God," he said.

"I don't want to be comforted," Marcie said. "I want to understand." She leaned forward. "Ever since I faced the truth the other day, there's been one awful question pounding away at me: *Why?* Not *Why me?* Because, God knows, I don't wish this on anyone else, but why anyone? Oh, I know that man is responsible for the evil in the world. Crime, war, hatred—they're human creations, and if they exist and we suffer from them, it's because we ourselves perpetuate them. But man isn't responsible for disease and early death." She put a hand to her head. "Man's not responsible for things like this."

"Honey, please," Robert said, "you're making things worse for yourself."

She pulled her hand away. "No, Bob! I have to know. I have to understand."

Rabbi Klein ran a hand over his thinning gray hair. Under his jacket, his arm still bore the number tatooed in Auschwitz. "You're asking a question that Jews have asked for six thousand years. In all that time, no one has come up with a definitive answer. The whole Book of Job is devoted to it, and even that doesn't tell us why we suffer, but it shows us how God expects us to bear our suffering so that it will ennoble, not degrade, us."

"Then the Book of Job falls short, and so does God," Robert said, his face feeling hot. "Maybe He doesn't exist at all. What kind of benevolent God would cut someone like Marcie down in full bloom?"

"Certainly not the kind of God you seem to have in mind—an old man with a long, white beard who doles out candy-coated lives like a benevolent grandfather." The rabbi shook his head and smiled sadly. "Surely, after all the years you spent in religious school as a boy and in the synagogue as a man, you know that isn't our God, Robert."

"I know, I know!" Impatience frosted Robert's voice. "God is His word, His laws. We're supposed to find Him only through living the righteous life of Torah, by doing justly, loving mercy, and walking humbly with Him. That sounds so sane, so logical, when things are going right. But it falls apart when things are going wrong."

"No, that precept doesn't fall apart when things go wrong," the rabbi said quietly. "*We* fall apart."

He looked from Robert to Marcie. "Maybe it's because we've read so many fairy tales when we're young—or maybe it's something inherently tied up with human frailty—but we all seem to be guilty of making the assumption that we're entitled to live happily ever after, that life is supposed to be a smooth road that we should be able to skip joyfully along. Whenever evil, sorrow, or tragedy waylay us along the way, we react with hurt surprise, as though they are out of place and out of order and have no relation to the real business of living."

Marcie sat forward a little, her face intent, but she said nothing.

"It is we who are out of order in reacting that way," Rabbi Klein went on. "Life holds no guarantee of uninterrupted happiness. Our American forefathers recognized that when they wrote that all men have a right to the pursuit of happiness—not to happiness itself. From its inception thousands of years ago, our religion has recognized that evil, heartbreak, sorrow, disappointment, and death are a part of life—not apart from it. In a way, the Torah is centered around that concept, for its purpose is to teach man how to live—how to deal with everything life brings him, not just how to cope with joy."

Her eyes never leaving the rabbi's face, Marcie gripped Robert's hand. "Yes, yes," she said a little breathlessly. "That's right. What's happening to me is just a part of life, isn't it? I'm not unique. It has happened to others before me, and it will happen to others after me. And it has happened and will go on happening not for some obscure or profound reason, but simply because it is a part of the mixture of good and bad, happiness and tragedy that makes up all life. And yet—" Her shoulders seemed to slump a bit, and some of the light went out of her face. "And yet, it's not easy . . . to die . . . young."

Rabbi Klein nodded. "I can't imagine that it is," he said. He sighed. "There's a Jewish folk saying, though, that translates, 'No man dies before his time.' What it means is that every life is complete when it ends. Each of us is given a certain amount of time on earth, and—whether it is six weeks, six years, or six decades—when that time is over, we have lived our complete life span, not had our life cut short."

Marcie looked pensive. "Yes," she said slowly, "that's true, isn't it?"

Robert was pleased that Marcie seemed to be finding some comfort in the rabbi's words, but his own rage against the death sentence his wife was living under had not been quelled. He lashed out at the rabbi as he would have liked to lash out at God.

"What if it is true that no life can be cut short before it is complete, that death, evil, and tragedy are all a part of living, and what if the Torah has grown out of that conception? What comfort is there in knowing that?"

"You know that if you're looking for palliatives, you won't find them in our religion," Rabbi Klein said softly. "Comfort? We don't need comfort in the worst of times. We need strength and support. That's what the Torah offers us—not comfort to wallow in, but strength and support to see us through."

"See us through?" Marcie's hand tightened on Robert's, and the serenity fled from her face. "No, not *us—you*. It can see *you* through, it can see Bob through, but what about me? Once I've been seen through this crisis, I won't be here anymore. It's not life I need help getting through—it's death."

The rabbi sighed, and, for a fleeting second, his eyes seemed to mirror the suffering of Jews of all time. "It's true. Ours is an earth-bound, life-centered religion. For the Jew, since the beginning of time, it is life that he has needed courage and strength to face and endure. In comparison to that, death has always been easy."

"It isn't easy for me," Marcie said.

"Of course not. It can't be easy for anyone who knows that his own death is imminent, but, actually, it's that last bit of death-overshadowed life that you need help facing, not the final act of death itself. And the Torah would tell you to live every moment allotted to you to its fullest, and to face the fact that there are not destined to be many moments with courage and dignity."

"And then what?"

The rabbi shook his head. "I'm not sure I follow you."

"After death—what? That's what frightens me more than dying—being dead. It's as though my blood turns to ice in my veins every time I think about it."

She began to shiver, and Robert slipped his arm around her.

"I wish I could offer you assurances of a golden, glorious afterlife, but you know we don't believe in heaven and hell, except inasmuch as every person makes his own right here on earth."

"I know. That's what makes it so frightening, knowing how I feel inside—so real, so alive—and knowing that it will all just suddenly be turned off like the final flick of a switch." She was still shivering. "I can't accept that."

"You don't have to." The rabbi leaned forward. "The Torah makes it clear that there are two kinds of immortality. On the one hand, there's the finite kind right here on earth, where we live on in the hearts and the memories of those who loved us; on the other, there's the infinite kind, where our souls return to God, Who created them. Because if we accept the fact that our body is created of the elements of the earth and returns to them after death, then it's also logical to assume that that unique, God-given spirit that sets each of us apart returns to its Creator too and becomes part of Him once more."

"And that's it?" Marcie asked softly. "That's all?"

"Isn't it enough," the rabbi asked, "to become one with the Creator?"

For a moment, their gazes remained locked. Then Marcie closed her eyes and dropped her head.

Her trembling slowed, then stopped. When she opened her eyes again, she looked more calm.

"I'd like to go home now," she told Robert. "Will you get our things?"

When he returned with their coats, he found Marcie and the rabbi just as he had left them. No one spoke until the three of them had reached the door of the study. Then the rabbi broke the silence.

"The Talmud tells the story of two ships," he said, "one leaving on a long voyage and the other returning from one. The people on shore took no notice of the one docking, but they gave the one that was leaving a rousing send-off, cheering and waving. Then a wise man among them chastised them, telling them they were foolish to rejoice over a ship that was setting out to sea and might face countless unknown dangers. They should, he said, rejoice instead over the ship that returned to port safely, bringing home all its passengers in peace.

"That, the Talmud tells us, is human nature. We rejoice when a child is born, even though we don't know what trials and hardships lie ahead of him, and we cry when an adult dies, even when he or she dies in peace, having completed his or her journey with the indestructible crown of a good name. We should, the rabbis tell us, do the opposite—weep for the child and rejoice for the adult."

He took Marcie's hand in both of his. "Marcia, unfortunately for all of us, your life is destined to be a short one, but, happily for you, you can look back over it with no regrets. In the few years I've been fortunate enough to know you, I've learned that you're a fine wife, a wonderful mother, a good daughter, sister, and friend. You've given of yourself not only to your loved ones, but to your community and to your fellow man as well." He paused a second, and when he spoke again, his voice had thickened with emotion. "Your life has truly been a blessing to all who have known you, and you will sail into port with a shipload of *mitzvot*. Never lose sight of that in the days to come."

"Thank you," Marcie said, her voice cracking. "I'll try to remember that."

Robert swallowed hard, his vision blurring. "I'm sorry if I—" he began, searching for words to apologize for some of the things he had said, but the rabbi cut him off with an understanding smile and a wave of his hand.

"Thank you," Robert said.

"There's a time for talk and a time for reflection," the rabbi said, taking one of their hands in each of his. "I hope you will both feel free to ask me to join you in either at any time. And always remember what Solomon wrote in the Song of Songs: 'Love is as strong as death.' God bless you both."

They walked home hand in hand, neither of them speaking.

When Robert returned after taking the babysitter home, he found Marcie seated in the rocker in the children's room, silhouetted in the dim glow of the night light that shone through the little door of a lamp that was fashioned to look like the home of the Old Woman Who Lived in a Shoe. He kissed the sleeping children, then went over to Marcie and slipped an arm around her shoulders.

"It's late," he said. "Let's go to bed."

She made no move to rise, but continued to rock gently to and fro.

"Oh, Bob! They're so little!" she whispered finally. "They need me so much. How can I bear to leave them when I love them so?"

He wanted to answer, but the tears in his throat drowned his words.

She leaned her head against him. "There was so much I wanted to tell Rachel as she was growing up, so many hurdles I wanted to help her over. And Benjie too. Now they'll have to grow up without me." Her shoulders shook as she drew a deep breath. "They're so young that they probably won't even remember me. They'll never know how much I love them."

"Yes, they will," Robert assured her, "because I won't let them forget you, and I'll tell them how much you loved them." He tightened his arm around her. "Come on now. It's late."

She rose slowly and walked with him, her head resting on his shoulder. On the threshold, she paused, straightened, and looked back at the two sleeping children.

"The other day," she said, "I let them go down the hall to play at Billy's house. They came back all full of questions because they'd found out

Billy's parakeet had died. I tried to explain death to them, trying to make it sound like something that shouldn't be frightening. I said it was a simple part of the life cycle that all God's creatures—from pets to parents—go through. They couldn't get my meaning, though. How could they? Death seems so remote to little children, and even adults don't understand it. They just kept asking why Billy's parakeet had to go away."

She paused, and when she spoke again, there was a tremble in her voice. "When the time comes, you'll tell them I didn't want to leave them, won't you? You'll make them see that I had no choice?"

"You know I will."

Gently, he closed the door behind them, then led her down the hall to their own room. He handed her her nightgown and robe and got out his own pajamas, but she made no move to undress. Instead, she sat down on the bed, her mind obviously still back with the children.

"No one could love them as I do," she said. "That's what hurts so much. Oh, I know another woman could and will love them—but not as I do. She could never love you as I do either."

Robert went cold. "What the hell are you talking about?"

"Your next wife."

"My God!" The air rushed out of him as though she'd punched him in the stomach, and he sank down on the bed beside her. "You know there could never be anyone else."

"No, I don't," she said, her eyes filling. "I know

that you could never love anyone else as I'm lucky enough to have you love me—not because I'm so special, but because what we have together is so special it could never be duplicated. But, someday, there may be someone else you can love in a different way."

"No." His lips felt numb as the word slipped through them. "No."

"Oh, God! Don't look at me that way!" She jumped up from the bed, her eyes flashing. "I'm not saying this out of some generous, noble impulse. I'm saying it because it has to be said. Because I know you're such a nut you might still feel married to me after I'm dead. And you won't be. God knows, I hate the thought of you with another woman. But that's because I'm still here and *able* to think. When I'm gone, all that will change. It won't matter anymore. That's what I have to keep reminding myself. And I have to remind you of that too. Not because I want you to love another woman—I'm too much of a selfish bitch for that—but because I don't want you to feel guilty if and when you do." She burst into tears.

"Honey, honey, don't!" Robert rushed over and took her in his arms.

"Why can't I be noble about it?" she sobbed against his chest. "Why do I have to be such a bitch?"

"You could never be a bitch," he whispered, "not even if you practiced for a hundred years. The very fact that you're not trying to make yourself look like a saint is the noblest thing you could do."

He buried his face in her hair. "I love you so much. I won't let you die. I won't let you go."

She looked up at him, trying to smile in her old teasing way. "Do you plan on wrestling with the Angel of Death?"

"If I could, I would win."

She slipped out of his arms, serious once more. "When the time comes, I don't plan on wrestling with him, and I don't want you to make me."

"I don't understand."

She turned back to him. "I want you to promise me that when the time comes, when I—when I go into the coma, you won't let anyone administer any life-prolonging techniques."

"No! My God! I love you. I want you with me every second possible. How can you ask me to cut your life short?"

"It's not my life you'd be cutting short, it's my death."

"No! I won't do it! As long as you're alive, there'll be hope."

"Hope of what—a lengthy death? Bob, we both know that the minute I go into that coma, I'm as good as dead."

"Stop it!" He sank down on the desk chair. "I don't want to talk about it!"

"We *have* to talk about it!"

"Not now!" His heart was pounding, rushing hot blood to his cheeks. He thought he was going to be sick.

"Yes, now!" Marcie insisted. "Tomorrow—even ten minutes from now—it may be too late."

"No!" He kept shaking his head.

"Bob, listen to me! *Please!* You've never had to watch someone you love die by dribs and drabs—I have. My father went into a coma before he died. For weeks, he lay in a hospital bed with more needles in him than a pincushion and more tubes running through him than a mad scientist's laboratory. And for what? So that day by day we could watch death nibble away at him, changing him from the laughing, loving man we knew into a monstrous sleeping skeleton—"

"Stop it!" He leapt from the chair, his whole body trembling.

"No! Not until you promise!" She took his hands in hers. "This isn't any spur-of-the-moment idea. I've been thinking about it since I learned the truth. I've already spoken to Dr. Halpern about it. I'm supposed to go to his office on Monday and sign a paper. But what if something happens before then? Or what if he's out of town when I go into the coma, or there are other complications? Then, as my husband, you'll have the final say about my treatment. I've got to know that your say will be the same as mine."

Marcie's face blurred as he met her half-demanding, half-begging gaze. "But I love you!" he protested.

"All the more reason to do this one last thing for me. The rabbi said tonight that I should live what little life is left to me with dignity. Please, *please,* Bob, promise me you'll help me die with dignity too."

He pulled her so close he could feel her heart pounding against his. "All right." He forced the words past the fist in his throat. "I promise."

He felt her relax in his arms. "Thank you," she whispered. "I love you." He could feel her tears on his neck. "Remember that promise, because I'll never bring it up again. Death can have me for eternity, but we have only a little while. I'm going to concentrate on that from now on."

Chapter Five

Roscoe Bradcliff presented all the tenured members of the English department and ranking officers of the administration with autographed copies of his latest anthology at the faculty Christmas party. The inscriptions ranged—in order of the influence of the recipients—from warm paeans to unceremonial signatures. It was with one of the latter unglorified copies that he approached Robert.

"Well, so here you are, Robert!" he said with forced joviality.

Robert glanced down at his feet and then up again. "Yes, so I am!" he said as though pleasantly surprised that they'd both found him in the same place.

Bradcliff displayed the copy of his book in front of his chest as though he were participating in a game of show-and-tell. "I have a little something for you." His tone and countenance, of course, made it clear that what he had was far from little and a great deal more than merely something.

"Are you sure that's for me, Roscoe? I haven't received my tenure yet—or do you know something I don't know?"

"Well, as a matter of fact—" Bradcliff's eyes sparkled conspiratorially. He slipped an arm around Robert's shoulders, heading him away from the punch bowl, obviously playing the part of a secret agent about to impart a Great Confidence. "I guess it's all right to let the cat out of the bag. You know how hard I've been working for you. Well, I finally managed to pull things off in your favor this morning."

"No kidding?" He tried not to show how relieved he felt.

"You'll be getting official word any day now. Of course, I don't want you to think it was easy!"

"Believe me, I'd be the last person to think that."

"But I was in there plugging for you all the way." He landed a mock punch on Robert's shoulder. "I like to give you young fellas all the help I can."

"I appreciate it."

He pressed the book into Robert's hand. "Well, this is my way of saying 'welcome aboard.' "

"Hello, Bradcliff. You telling Silver all the good things we heard about him the other day?"

Bradcliff's face froze in mid-smile. "Hello, Dowley. I didn't see you."

"You rarely do." He turned his sharp eyes on Robert. "Roscoe and I had a very pleasant chitchat with the representative your publisher sent to the annual meeting of the Chaucer Society the other night, didn't we, Roscoe?"

Bradcliff's face flushed with anger.

"Nice young fella, wasn't he, Roscoe? All full of talk about how the big boys back at his office are predicting great things for your book when it comes out in the spring, Robert. Seems they think that the new light you shed on the old girl's love life will chalk up big sales and initiate a revival of her works. Now don't tell me you forgot to mention that to Robert, Roscoe!"

"We had more important things to talk about than vague prognostications about the future. Now, if you'll excuse me." He pushed his way through the crowd.

Dowley raised his punch glass to Bradcliff's retreating back, then took a sip, grimacing. "When will they learn that cheap punch does nothing to enhance the flavor of cheap wine, and vice versa?" He turned his gaze back to Robert. "It looks like you're going to be an Important Man to Know around here soon."

Robert was too aware of the reading public's unpredictability to take fire. "I'll believe it when I see it," he said.

"Bradcliff believes it. After talking to that guy, he couldn't get his ass back here fast enough to change his tenure vote on you. Watch him. If his next anthology isn't Wharton short stories and if he doesn't ask you to write an introduction to it, I'll comb your beard for a month."

Robert laughed. "That's some wager. If I win, I lose."

"Just like life." He glanced around the room. "Where's the Lorelei of the literary set? She's usually breathing down your neck."

"Katherine? She has bigger fish to fry now. She's up for tenure next term, and I'm not on any of the committees. The last time I saw her, she had latched on to Dean Wilson of the personnel and budget committee."

"Pity."

"For him, not for me."

Dowley downed the rest of his punch. "Want some more of this vile stuff?"

"No, thanks. I had my token drink and put in my token appearance. I'm going to shove off."

"Well, I think I'll have a few more for the road."

Before Robert had reached the lounge door, Dowley was back, grabbing his arm.

"Christ! Graystone has a bun on. He's at the punch bowl, lining up everyone he can get his hands on for one of his readings. Let's get the hell out of here!"

They hurried to their offices for their coats.

In the street, they turned their collars up against an icy wind whose dampness promised snow.

"Good Riviera weather," Dowley grumbled.

"Is that where you're headed for during vacation?"

He shook his head. "My travelling days are over. The world holds no surprises. There's no place to hide and nothing new to find."

"A lot of people wouldn't agree with that."

"The more fools they." He lowered his head against the wind. "I knew a guy once who'd never been away from Manhattan. He was crazy to travel, but couldn't afford it. So he entered every goddam contest that offered trips as prizes. After years and years, he finally drew fourth prize in one—a weekend in New York City. He nearly blew his brains out."

"It was better than nothing."

"Not when you've had your heart set on London, Paris, or Rome. He told the contest people to shove it."

With a shrug, Robert turned to say good-bye at the subway entrance.

He had a long wait for his train, and, as he paced the platform, his breath trailing him in little frosted puffs, he thought about Dowley's friend and the weekend he'd thrown away. The man had been a shithead not to take it. He and Marcie had always longed to travel too, but if they—

Suddenly, his mind shifted gears and began racing uphill. A train roared into the station, but he pushed his way out of the group crowding around its unopened doors and ran upstairs to the phone booth near the turnstiles. He dialled information, then dialled the number he received.

When he went back down to the subway platform a little while later, he was feeling happy for the first time in months.

Marcie was alone in her studio when he got home, the children having gone to play with friends.

"How's it going?" He planted a kiss on her neck.

"Not so good." She put down her brushes and paints and began to wipe her hands with a turpentine rag. Because she'd begun having difficulty with her vision, she'd had to turn down work for Bambi Books, and she spent her spare time working on a portrait of the children.

"I ought to give up on this," she said. "I don't know whether it's my eyes or my touch or both, but I can't seem to capture them."

Robert eyed the canvas and saw what she meant. "It will come," he said.

"No, it won't." It was a simple statement of fact—wistful, perhaps, but not bitter. She had been true to the word she had given him on the night he had given her his promise. "How was the big bash?"

"The usual—rotten punch, rotten company. I got a present, though." He exhibited Bradcliff's book.

"Hey! The door prize for the men's room. What did you do to rate it?"

"Oh," he said with hammed-up nonchalance, "Bradcliff just happens to like the way I part my beard."

"The hell he does! That bastard always has a

good reason if he parts with one of his books without palming the cold cash."

"Well, there was something. A couple of things. As a matter of fact, I have three surprises for you."

"Three! That's a bumper crop." Her eyes sparkled. "Come on. You know I can't stand suspense."

"I'll report them in order of increasing importance. First, I've been voted tenure."

She threw her arms around him. "Oh, honey! That's wonderful! I knew it would come through for you. It had to."

"Well, I wasn't so sure. People who have a hell of a lot more to offer than I do have been refused."

"No one has more to offer than you do. When did it happen? How did you find out? No, wait! Surprises first, details later. What's the next surprise?"

"Word's out in the business that my publisher expects big things of my book—sales that will go beyond the usual literary circles."

She laughed with delight, hugging him. "You see? Haven't I told you so all along?" She pulled away a little so that she could look at him. "You know, so far, you've given me good news, but no surprises. After all, you can't call sure things surprises. The next one better be good, mister."

"It's your anniversary present."

"But our anniversary isn't until Saturday."

He touched her cheek. "It's not the sort of thing I can gift wrap. We're spending the weekend at the Plaza."

"Now *that*," she whispered, her eyes misting, "*is* a surprise."

He pulled her close. "Happy anniversary, honey."

They left late Friday afternoon after a dozen hugs and kisses from Rachel and Benjie, who were being looked after by Sarah.

Down in the street, Robert tried to hail a cab, but the few that whizzed by were either occupied or off duty. After a frigid five-minute wait, Marcie insisted that they take the subway.

"Benjie's peanut-butter kisses have turned to ice on my cheeks," she said, "and the rest of me is about to join them."

Shaking his head, Robert picked up their valise. "I'm sure most of the Plaza's guests don't arrive via the New York City Transit System."

Laughing, Marcie slipped her arm through his. "They don't know what they're missing!"

When they emerged from the subway at Lexington Avenue and Fifty-ninth Street, Marcie again vetoed a taxi.

"You can ride me home in style if you want," she said, "but I want the joy of approaching the Plaza slowly, relishing every step."

They paused in front of the Christmas-garlanded Fountain of Abundance that faced the hotel, taking in the building in all its majesty.

"There she stands," Robert said, "the last holdout of the Age of Elegance."

"Long may she wave."

"Amen."

They crossed the street and entered the hotel, evading the doorman, who was ministering to the door-opening needs of an elegant-looking couple in an Alfa-Romeo.

In the lobby, they paused for a moment, noting the tasteful nod the Plaza gave to the holiday season—a meticulously decorated Christmas tree and a display of prize-winning confections whose elegance rivalled the crystal chandeliers, Oriental rugs, potted palms, and marble staircases.

They crossed the floor to the desk, where Marcie stood by Robert's side as he registered.

"Enjoy your stay, sir," the clerk said, then rang a bell.

Instantly, a bellhop in green appeared.

The clerk handed him a key. "See Dr. and Mrs. Silver to room thirteen thirty-nine."

A white-gloved operator closed the gilded gates of his wood-panelled elevator and delivered them to the thirteenth floor. They stepped out onto the carpeted elevator corridor and through the glass, Plaza-crested door held open for them by the bell-hop. Then they followed him through the chan-deliered hallway to room 1339.

"Two threes and a multiple thereof—it's bound to be lucky," Marcie said, passing into the room.

After placing their valise on a suitcase rack and showing them the bathroom and the closet, the bellhop thanked Robert for his tip and left.

Marcie looked around the room, her eyes sparkling. A chandelier was suspended from the high ceiling, its crystal pendants throwing glittering reflections on the pale-green, white-panelled walls. The carpet and drapes were pale green too, as was the satin bedspread with its lace overlay that hid from view for the moment the sumptuous quilt and four overstuffed goose-down pillows it covered. There was also a wing chair, a gleamingly polished nightstand, and a mirrored vanity with a velvet-bottomed chair. A nineteenth-century print of a New York scene hung above the bed. The only visible concessions to the twentieth century were the push-button telephone on the night table and the television set, which, on private channels, provided viewing of current films.

Marcie shook her head. "I can't believe we're really here."

She went to inspect the bathroom. "Look at this!" she called. "Wall-to-wall towels—and a phone too!"

"You look like a kid let loose in a toy shop."

"I feel like one." She hugged him. "I love you!"

"Care to prove it?"

"Try and stop me."

Carefully, they removed the elegant spread from the bed. Then they showed the stately Victorian walls what twentieth-century love was like.

Later, when the first wintry stars bored their way through the frozen sky, they showered together in the old-fashioned tub, towelled each other till their bodies glowed with warmth and love, dressed, and went out for the evening. After seeing a wacky English comedy in a first-run theater, they ate dinner in the same noisy but excellent French restaurant they had frequented during their dating days and the early years of their marriage, before the children had come and tied them closer to home.

"We're not having dessert," Robert informed Marcie when he had packed away the last of his ragout.

"But we ordered the complete dinner, and I love their pies!"

He shook his head. "I have something else in mind."

Shrugging, she put down her napkin and slipped into her coat.

The something else he had in mind was dessert in the Palm Court of the Plaza. There, they sipped demitasse and ate the strawberry tarts they had selected from the pastry display, listening to a string trio play schmaltz tunes until around eleven o'clock, when Marcie's eyes lost some of their sparkle and began to show fatigue.

Back in their room, Marcie seemed to fall asleep almost before her head sank into the delicious depths of her pillows.

She was still asleep when Robert awoke at eight o'clock the following morning. He dressed quietly and slipped from the room. A half-hour later, he returned, knocking at the door, rather than opening it with his key.

"Who is it?" Marcie asked, her voice still thick with sleep.

"Room service, madam."

Laughing, she opened the door. "I'd know that

phony French accent anywhere. Happy anniversary, honey."

He drew her close and kissed her. "Happy anniversary." When he released her, he turned her around. "Now, back to bed."

"Why?"

"Because madam is about to partake of breakfast in bed at the Plaza."

While she climbed back into bed, he went into the bathroom and pulled one of the towels from the racks. Returning, he spread it over her lap. Then he produced from the bag he carried the container of coffee and the jelly doughnut he had purchased at a nearby luncheonette.

"This," Marcie said through a mouthful of doughnut, "is sheer luxury!" With an elegance worthy of the queen of England herself, she transferred a drop of jelly from chin to pinky to tongue. "My compliments to the chef."

While she consumed the remainder of her breakfast, Robert sat on the edge of the bed, and they planned their day.

That day began at nine-thirty when they left the Plaza and strolled along Fifth Avenue to Temple Emanu-El where they attended sabbath services, holding hands and feeling as though the rabbi's benediction at the end was for them alone. Afterward, they shopped for presents for Sarah and the children, then had a leisurely lunch, which was followed by a visit to the Frick Museum, one of Marcie's favorites.

They had planned to see a movie in the late

afternoon, but by four o'clock, Marcie looked so weary that Robert suggested they return to the hotel and rest before dinner. To ensure that she would be undisturbed, he left her alone in their room and walked over to the Donnell Library, where he browsed and read.

Finding her still asleep when he returned at six, he sat quietly in the armchair near the window and watched the people hurrying across the Grand Army Plaza in the glow of the city's lights. It was nearly seven when she stirred and turned on the bedside lamp.

"It's so late! Why didn't you wake me?" she asked, blinking her eyes to adjust to the light.

"There's plenty of time. Society never dines before eight anyway."

"I'll have to tell my stomach that. It has very plebeian hunger pangs." She crawled to the end of the bed where she could reach the phone. "Let's call the children before we dress. How can I love being here alone with you and miss them so much at the same time?"

"Because you're such a rotten mother." Robert ducked the pillow tossed at him as he went into the bathroom to pick up the extension.

As they had been when Marcie and Robert had spoken to them that morning and the previous evening, Benjie and Rachel were bubbling with questions. The information that their parents had two push-button phones, one of which was in the bathroom, seemed to impress them most of all.

After the final telephone kisses had been sent

and received, Marcie and Robert showered and changed. Then they stood side by side, looking at their image in the mirror above the vanity—Robert in his all-purpose dark suit, white shirt, and wide, colorful tie, Marcie in her floor-length black-velvet skirt and low-cut pink angora sweater.

"Who could guess," Robert asked with a slight bow toward their reflection, "that we're not visiting nobility?"

"We could certainly fool me."

He crooked his arm. "May I have the honor of escorting you to dinner?"

"Charmed." She slipped her hand through his arm. "But won't we take cold, Lord Bottomly, walking through the streets without any cloaks?"

"Not at all, my dear Lady Vanderrock, because your dainty foot will not come in contact with the street. Tonight we dine at the Plaza."

A few minutes later, the maître d'hôtel was leading them to a table for two that overlooked Central Park. There, in the glow of candlelight reflected on snowy linen and richly panelled walls, they celebrated their tenth anniversary with champagne cocktails and a sumptuous five-course meal.

By the end of the meal, Marcie's cheeks were glowing and her eyes sparkling with an animation that had not lighted them for a long time.

"It's only ten," Robert said, reaching for her hand. "What would you like to do now?"

"Be alone with you."

"That's the best idea of the weekend."

He paid the waiter, and then they walked through the lobby to the elevator.

As soon as they'd closed the door to their room behind them, Marcie threw her arms around him.

"Oh, Bob! I feel so good!" she said. "I can't remember the last time I felt so good!"

She slipped from his arms and flipped on the light switch. "I want to call the children and say good night."

"Honey, it's after ten. They've been asleep for hours."

"Maybe not. Maybe Mom let them stay up late because we're away, or maybe they can't sleep. I only want to talk to them for a minute. I just want to hear their voices again."

He shook his head and smiled as she picked up the phone and punched out their number.

"Hello, Mom? It's me. . . . No, I'm fine. Everything's fine. In fact, everything's wonderful." She turned to Robert and blew him a kiss. "I just thought I'd call and say good night to the children. . . . You're sure? Maybe they're down but not out. Would you check? . . . I know it's silly, but—well, I just feel like talking to them, that's all." She picked up a pencil and began to doodle while she waited for Sarah to return to the phone.

"You're a nut, you know that?" Robert teased, taking off his jacket and loosening his tie.

She stuck out her tongue, then went back to her doodling. "Hi. . . . Oh, they are." Her voice dipped down with disappointment, but her pencil continued to slip across the paper. "No, you were right not to wake them. . . . I guess I was being silly. . . . Okay, I will. I tell you what, though. When they get up in the morning, tell them I called—and tell them I love them. . . . Right. See you tomorrow. Good night, Mom, and thanks for everything."

She replaced the receiver and put down the pencil with a little shrug. "Well, so much for mad flights of impetuosity."

"I had one of those while you were sleeping this afternoon. It led me straight to a liquor store for this." He reached into the closet and brought out a bottle.

"Harvey's Bristol Cream! You really are intent on spoiling me rotten."

"And myself in the process." He started to open the bottle.

"No, not yet. Let's get comfortable first. But you take your things into the bathroom and change, and don't come out till I call you. I have a little surprise of my own."

"Sounds interesting." He took his pajamas and robe and disappeared into the bathroom.

"Now?" he called out a few minutes later.

"Now."

He came out carrying the two bathroom tumblers, but he nearly dropped them when he saw Marcie, the light from the lamp outlining her curves through the graceful Grecian lines and gossamer folds of a turquoise nightgown. Her hair cascaded over her shoulders, shining as brightly as her eyes.

"You're even more lovely than you were ten

years ago," he said, but his voice caught a little on the words as he noticed how much thinner and how much paler she was too.

He held up the tumblers. "The hotel was kind enough to provide us with sherry glasses."

"How like the Plaza!"

He poured the sherry and handed her a glass, searching his mind for an appropriate toast. On past anniversaries, they had always drunk to the future, but now . . .

Evidently sensing his hesitation, Marcie raised her own glass. "Happy anniversary," she said simply. "*L'chaim.*"

He touched his glass to hers. "Yes," he said, "*l'chaim*—to life and to love and to the girl who taught me that they're one and the same."

They drank.

Smiling, she reached out and touched his cheek. "Hey!" she said. "If you're going to be a maudlin drunk, I'll take your drink away."

He grabbed her hand before she could remove it, holding it to his cheek for a moment. It felt warm and soft beneath his fingers—and thin, so very thin. Slowly, he turned his face until his lips met her palm.

Her eyes were sparkling. "I mean it, Bob," she said. "You can't be sad—not when I'm so happy. Can't you sense it? Something wonderful has happened this weekend. I feel better than I have for months. I haven't had any pain, any nausea. My vision hasn't blurred once." She gripped his hand. "Don't you realize what that means? It means it's stopped growing—maybe even started to shrink." Her cheeks flushed and her words tumbled over each other in excitement. "There have been cases like that. I've read about them. The doctors don't know why or how they happen, but they do. Oh, honey! The nightmare is over. I can feel it."

He gripped her hand, searching her face, his heart pounding half in hope, half in fear. *God! Let it be true!* "Are you sure?" It was more a plea than a question.

She closed her eyes and threw her head back in ecstasy. "Yes, yes, yes! A person who's dying can't possibly feel so alive. Bob, we're going to live and love for a long, long time. We'll laugh and love and work and love some more. And I'm going to paint pictures the likes of which you've never seen. The first thing I'm going to do when we get home is start one of the square down there."

Slipping her hand from his, she rushed to the window and drew up the blind. "I'm going to paint it just as we see it from this window. I'm—" She stopped, gazing down at the street. "It's snowing! Oh, look at all that snow!" She turned to him, her face as soft as the snowflakes fluttering past their window. "It's a sign, Bob. I can feel it. A sign that what I'm feeling now is as pure and true as the snow. I *am* getting well. We *will* be together always—I promise you that."

"Thank God." There were tears in his eyes as well as his voice as he walked over and slipped his arms around her shoulders.

He switched off the lamp, and they stood at the

window for a long time, watching the snow float past, lighting the darkness with its blue-white glow. Every flake seemed to hold a promise of its own.

Suddenly, Marcie laughed, her eyes lighting with mischief. "Do you know what else that snow means?"

"From the look in your eyes, I'm almost afraid to ask."

"It means that tomorrow morning, we're going to Central Park to have a snowball fight. And I'm going to beat the pants off you."

"You sound pretty damn sure of yourself."

"I've got pretty good aim."

"You couldn't hit the side of a billboard if it shook hands with you."

"We'll see about that tomorrow."

"Okay. And the loser gets her face washed in snow."

"Don't be so sure about the sex of the loser!"

"There's no question about it. In fact," he said, opening the window and grabbing a handful of snow from the sill, "I'm so sure that you might as well pay the forfeit now."

"No fair!" she laughed and dashed away from him.

They scrambled around the room, hitting a standoff when she ducked behind the chair. With a growl worthy of the abominable snowman, Robert pulled the chair out of the way and cornered her near the bed. By then, the snow had melted, so he dipped one finger in the puddle in his palm and touched it to her nose.

"Uncle?" he asked, wiping his hand on his robe.

"Uncle," she said, laughing.

His gaze went from her eyes to her lips and back again. "Oh, God! How I love you!" he said.

She went into his arms.

Robert had thought that in the ten years they had been married, they had experienced all of love's pleasures. He was wrong. That night, catapulted from the depths of old love to the heights of new hope, he and Marcie scaled mountains of delight they hadn't dreamed existed.

Later—much later—deliciously exhausted, they fell asleep, Marcie with her cheek nestled in the hair of his chest, he with his hand gently encompassing her breast.

Once, during the night, he awoke to find Marcie propped on one elbow, looking down at him.

"I'm glad you're awake," she whispered. "I wanted to tell you how happy you make me and how much I love you."

He smiled sleepily, gently touching her hair. "You've told me that a million times."

"That's not nearly enough. I wanted to say it again, to hear it again."

"I love you," he whispered, drawing her head back to his chest, "love you, love you. . . ." He repeated the words until they were both asleep once more.

Sunlight streaming through the windows awoke Robert around eight the next morning. He slipped from bed and looked out at the snow-covered city that awaited them.

"Hey, come on, sleepyhead! We have a date in the park, remember?" he called.

Marcie didn't answer.

"Up and at 'em," he said, walking back toward the bed.

Marcie didn't stir, not even to put the pillow over her head as she usually did.

"Chickening out, eh?" He reached down to whip off the covers and tickle her, but stopped midway, feeling as though an icy hand had wiped the smile from his lips, then reached inside him to get a stranglehold on his heart. "Marcie?"

She lay still and quiet. Too still, too quiet.

"Marcia?" He wet his lips. "Come on, honey. It's time to get up. We're going to the park, remember?"

He shook her gently, then desperately. Her body reacted limply, like a rag doll being shaken by a frantic child.

"Marcie, wake up! Please! Please! Remember what you said last night? Remember, you said the nightmare was over. Over. Oh, my God! Marcie!"

The excruciating pain behind his eyes sought release in a rush of tears as he gathered her to him, burying his face between her breasts. He held her that way for a long time—until he began to hear the soft, slow beat of her heart above his sobs. Tenderly, he lay her back on her pillow. He picked up her nightgown from the floor, where she'd tossed it with such abandon the night before, and gently slipped it on her.

He found his wallet, searched through it for

Halpern's card, then punched out the number on the phone.

An answering service greeted him.

"This is an emergency," he said. "I have to speak to Dr. Halpern."

"He's away on vacation. His patients are being cared for by Dr. John Roth," the operator told him. She gave him Dr. Roth's number.

He pounded the number out on the phone and was greeted by another answering service. Dr. Roth, he was told, was away for the weekend, but he had left the number of Dr.— he hung up before the operator had a chance to finish.

His hand trembling, he pressed the button for the desk.

"Good morning. May I help you?" The clerk's voice was cool and efficient. He had to ask his question twice more before Robert could answer it.

"Yes. This is Robert Silver in thirteen thirty-nine. I—" He closed his eyes and swallowed. "My wife is very sick. We—she needs a doctor right away."

"I'll contact one for you immediately, sir."

"Thank you." As he replaced the receiver, the note pad by the phone caught his eye—the one Marcie had been doodling on the night before when she wanted to talk to the children. Only, instead of idle doodles, it bore a magnificent sketch of Rachel and Benjie. In a few brief strokes on a scratch pad, Marcie had captured the very essence of their children's souls.

He couldn't be sure how long he had been staring at the picture through his tears when he heard a knock on the door. He threw on his robe and let the doctor in.

A suave man in his late fifties, the doctor looked more like he should be carrying an attaché case than a medical bag. "What seems to be the matter?" he asked, approaching the bed.

While Robert explained Marcie's condition, the doctor examined her quickly and efficiently.

"She's in a coma," he said. "She'll have to be moved to a hospital."

"Is there a chance she'll come out of it?"

The doctor shook his head. "From what you told me, I thought you understood that."

"I do." Robert looked away. "I just don't want to."

The doctor picked up the phone and began punching some numbers. "You'd better get some clothes on," he said.

Robert nodded and went into the bathroom to dress.

When the ambulance attendants arrived, the doctor opened the door for them. He spoke to them briefly, and then they turned their attention to Marcie. With one quick movement, they had her off the bed and on the stretcher, a heavy blanket strapped around her.

"Will you follow in your car or ride with us?" one of them asked Robert.

"I'll ride with you." He tore the picture from the note pad, slipped it into his pocket, and followed them out the door.

At the Plaza, even illness and death must conduct themselves with the proper decorum. There is no room for them in the glass-and-wood-panelled elevators or beneath the lobby's crystal chandeliers. They must slip swiftly and silently through the halls to the service elevator and leave through the service entrance, hiding themselves from view like dark Victorian secrets.

Though his legs felt weighted down with lead, Robert forced them to keep up with the ambulance attendants as they followed that path.

"Do you want to ride in back?" one of them asked after they had secured the stretcher inside the ambulance.

He nodded and climbed in.

The doors closed behind him with a soft, sickening thud of finality. There was no need for full-blast sirens; emergencies exist only where there is hope.

"Oh, Marcie, Marcie!" he whispered, brushing her hair back from her face. "When we said we'd ride away from the Plaza, we didn't mean like this."

He watched as the Plaza receded from view, snow as white as its linens clinging to it and icicles as bright as its chandeliers glinting on its canopy like gigantic frozen tears.

Three times before he'd ridden to hospitals by Marcie's side. But then it had been in taxicabs, and twice they'd returned with new life in their arms. The last time, though, they'd come out with Death at their heels, and now he was beckoning them back.

With a trembling hand, he smoothed the sheet under Marcie's chin, remembering how she'd looked the night she'd begged him not to let the doctors prolong her life.

"But I love you," he whispered now. "I want you with me as long as I can have you—even if it has to be this way. Surely, you can understand that."

Was it so wrong, he wondered, to want to keep her with him any way he could? Yet he knew that if it wasn't wrong, it was selfish. And selfishness was something Marcie had never given in to. All through her last weeks, she'd put him first, keeping up her spirits so that he could keep up his. Wasn't it time he put her first? He closed his eyes over his tears. Could he bring himself to do it?

At the hospital, he followed the attendants as they wheeled Marcie down a long tiled hall, but they stopped him, insisting he must report to the admitting office to fill out forms.

In the office, he was told Miss Caruth would take care of him. He sat in the chair before her vacant desk and looked around. There were two other desks in the immediate area. At one, a middle-aged woman sat typing. A girl in her early twenties was perched on the edge of the other, talking to its occupant—who was about the same age—about last night's date. Both wore slacks and elaborate eye make-up and, between their gossip and giggles, sipped coffee from cardboard containers.

After several minutes, the girl who was on the desk stood up, stretched, and ambled over to Robert. She took the card an attendant had given him, casting a bored glance at it. Then she looked at him, her eyes totally disinterested.

"You a relative?"

"Husband."

Sighing, she sat down at the desk and shuffled papers around in slow motion until she had found the appropriate forms. She dropped her pen, and, as she came up from retrieving it from the floor, she examined her long red-painted fingernails, obviously finding a nick in one of them. She cast an annoyed glance in Robert's direction. If he hadn't been there, her nail would still be perfect.

After another sigh, she brushed invisible dust from the form before her. "Patient's last name?" she droned as if the name wasn't on the card before her.

"Silver."

"First."

"Marcia."

"Middle."

"Rose."

"Maiden name."

"Resnick."

"Address."

"One eighteen Eastern Parkway. Look, my wife's very sick. I'd like to be with her for a while. I have to see—" His tongue seemed to grow thick and to stumble on his words. He took a breath and tried again. "I have to see that—that her wishes are carried out. Couldn't we fill this out later?"

"Sorry," she said, obviously not. "Phone number?"

He sighed and told her.

"Occupation?"

"I teach at—"

She jerked her head up. *Not you, dummy!* her eyes said. "Your *wife's* occupation."

"Oh. Free-lance artist."

She twisted her lips in scornful dismissal, but wrote it down. "Age?"

"Thirty-two."

"How many full-term pregnancies?"

"Two."

"Any others?"

"Look, I don't see—"

"Any others?"

"No."

"Religion?"

"Jewish."

"Is she covered by hospitalization insurance or any other medical insurance?"

"Yes, we have—"

"Does she have her own policy, or is she covered under yours?"

"Mine. I have—"

"May I see the cards, please?"

She drummed her fingers on the edge of her desk while Robert, his head pounding so hard he couldn't see straight, fumbled through his wallet for his cards. She took them and copied the information from them slowly, like a child just learning writing skills.

She returned the cards. "Your name."

A scream of rage was building up inside him. "It was on the cards."

"I didn't need them for that purpose. Your name, please."

"Robert Jacob Silver. I live at the same address, have the same phone, am associate professor of English at Seward College, which is part of the City University, am also Jewish, and have never been pregnant."

She shot him a murderous look. "A little more slowly, please. And answer the questions in the order I ask them."

He gripped the arms of his chair until his knuckles turned white. "Certainly."

One by one, they went through the questions. Then, after securing his signature on a consent form, Miss Caruth made a phone call.

"Your wife is in room fourteen-o-four," she said when she hung up. "Take the left bank of elevators."

He jumped from the chair like a prisoner released from his chains.

He went in the wrong direction first on the fourteenth floor, but he soon found room 1404. There were two beds in the room, one unoccupied, the other surrounded by a curtain. He pulled the curtain aside. Then, with a curse, he whirled and rushed out of the room and down to the nurses' station.

"Goddam it!" he said to the startled nurse on duty. "I'm Marcia Silver's husband. Who gave you permission to put all those tubes and needles in her?"

"Why, the doctor in charge of the floor, sir."

"Screw the doctor in charge of the floor! My wife doesn't want them in her. Take them out."

"Your wife's in no state to tell us that."

"No, but she was in a state to tell me and her own doctor a while back."

The nurse flashed him a starchy, professional smile. "Then I'm sure her own doctor will straighten everything out when he arrives."

"Dammit! Don't talk to me like I'm a mental defective! Her doctor's away on vacation. I don't know when he'll be back. I want you to take those things out of her now."

"I can't." The nurse was bristling too. "I take my orders from doctors only. Until your own doctor arrives, your wife is under the care of the resident on this floor."

"Then get him here, dammit."

The nurse walked leisurely from the desk, glaring over her shoulder at him. Some ten minutes later, she returned with a man in a white jacket.

"This is the husband of the woman in fourteen-o-four," she said.

"Hi," the doctor said. "We're doing everything we can for your wife. We've contacted Dr. Borden of neurology. He doesn't come in on Sundays, but he'll be around to take a look at her first thing tomorrow morning. Unless, of course, you have your own doctor."

"We do—Dr. Halpern—but he's away on vacation now."

"Halpern—Halpern? Is he a neuro man?"

"No, he's an internist, but he's been in contact with neurologists about my wife's case."

"Oh, a g.p." The doctor gave a shrug of dismissal. "Then you'll want to keep Dr. Borden on the case even after your own guy gets back. Borden's about the best there is."

"I'm sure he is, but I think you'll agree that even the best doctor can do"—Robert swallowed, trying to keep his voice from breaking—"do nothing for my wife at this stage."

"If you mean can we cure her—probably not. But we'll do everything we can to keep her alive as long as possible."

Robert ran his hand over his face. "That's exactly what we don't want." He told the doctor of Marcie's wishes then and asked him to carry them out.

"That's out of the question and totally opposed to medical procedure."

"Dr. Halpern doesn't think so. He's prepared to go along with her wishes."

"Dr. Borden or I will talk to him when he gets here."

Robert took a deep breath, willing himself to be calm, realizing that every minute that passed with Marcie under the unwanted treatment made the termination of that treatment more difficult. "I just finished telling you that he's away on vacation. For all I know, he may not be back for weeks."

The doctor shrugged. "Then until he arrives, your wife will be under Dr. Borden's care, and until Dr. Borden arrives tomorrow, she'll be under my care and must have the treatment I prescribe. By the way, your doctor *is* affiliated with this hospital, isn't he?"

An icy pain began to creep up the back of Robert's neck and to diffuse over his skull. He ran his hand through his hair. "How the hell should I know? Besides, what difference does it make?"

"If he's not affiliated with this hospital, he can't treat your wife here."

"Good God! He's her doctor! He's—"

"Those are the rules. They're the same at every hospital." The doctor was growing visibly impatient.

"My wife is in there dying, and you want to discuss rules?"

"I neither want to nor intend to discuss treatment or rules with you. Look, I can understand your concern, but, believe me, whatever problem your doctor's possible nonaffiliation with this hospital creates will be taken up when he arrives here."

"God knows when that will be!" Robert held his hands stiffly at his sides, trying to control their trembling. "In the meantime, as my wife's next of kin, I insist that you remove all that equipment from her room."

The doctor shook his head. "I don't take orders

from laymen, Mr. Silver. I'm a doctor. My job is to preserve life, not to cut it off. The treatment I've prescribed for your wife stands."

Robert looked into the steely eyes and realized that it was useless to argue further. His shoulders slumping, he turned and started to walk away.

"Mr. Silver."

Robert turned.

"I'm sorry about your wife. I'll do everything I can for her."

The doctor's face had softened, and suddenly he looked very young. His image blurred in Robert's eyes.

"Everything but what she wants," Robert said, and he turned away again.

For a long time after he re-entered her room, Robert stood looking down at Marcie. She lay pale and limp under the white covers, her long, dark hair spread over the pillow, her beautiful nightgown replaced by a white hospital coat.

"I tried, sweetheart," he whispered.

He thought of Marcie's plea to die with dignity and of the ugly court hearings and uglier publicity that surrounded recent cases in which families had tried to secure such a death for loved ones. And he thought of how he longed to keep Marcie with him for every possible moment.

He reached out to touch her hair, but his hand stopped midway. Slowly, he drew it back. Then he walked over and closed the door.

He returned to the bed. Gently, but determinedly, he disconnected all the equipment with which Marcie had been surrounded. Then, bending down, he placed a kiss on each closed eyelid and on her pale lips.

He drew a chair to the side of the bed, sat down, and took her left hand in both of his. Tenderly, he fingered her smooth gold wedding band. He closed his eyes over his tears, and, for just a second, he saw a vision of Marcie as she had looked standing before the window of their room in the Plaza the night before. Once again, he saw her dark eyes glowing with love, her cheeks glowing with life. Once again, he heard her promising him that they'd be together always.

Shaking his head, he opened his eyes and looked down at his wife's still, peaceful face. Through his tear-distorted vision, her lips almost seemed to curve into the semblance of the shadow of a smile. And, in that moment, he understood what she had been telling him the night before.

He drew her hand up to his lips and kissed her fingertips. "I kept my promise, sweetheart," he whispered.

Somehow, he knew, she would keep hers.

THE MOST EAGERLY AWAITED SEQUEL IN HISTORY!

THE BOOK THAT BEGINS WHERE *LOVE STORY* ENDS . . .

Oliver's STORY

ERICH SEGAL

THE DAZZLING #1 BESTSELLER
IS NOW A PARAMOUNT MOTION PICTURE
STARRING
RYAN O'NEAL and CANDICE BERGEN

From the running track of New York's Central Park to the hushed executive suites of a mighty department store empire, from a snowy Massachusetts Christmas to a shattering moment of truth in exotic Hong Kong, the story of Oliver Barrett IV is a story of passion and principle—the story of a young man's journey out of sadness into love.

"Reading it, you'll forget everything else until you've finished the last page. What a rare storyteller."

The Detroit News

"An expertly crafted novel that will delight the vast audience that enjoyed its predecessor." *Cosmopolitan*

AVON/42564/$2.25

OLI 12-78